Widdershins

by Don Nigro

A SAMUEL FRENCH ACTING EDITION

FOUNDED 1830
NEW YORK HOLLYWOOD LONDON TORONTO
SAMUELFRENCH.COM

Copyright © 2009 by Don Nigro
ALL RIGHTS RESERVED

CAUTION: Professionals and amateurs are hereby warned that WID-DERSHINS is subject to a licensing fee. It is fully protected under the copyright laws of the United States of America, the British Commonwealth, including Canada, and all other countries of the Copyright Union. All rights, including professional, amateur, motion picture, recitation, lecturing, public reading, radio broadcasting, television and the rights of translation into foreign languages are strictly reserved. In its present form the play is dedicated to the reading public only.

The amateur and professional live stage performance rights to WIDDERSHINS are controlled exclusively by Samuel French, Inc., and licensing arrangements and performance licenses must be secured well in advance of presentation. PLEASE NOTE that amateur licensing fees are set upon application in accordance with your producing circumstances. When applying for a licensing quotation and a performance license please give us the number of performances intended, dates of production, your seating capacity and admission fee. Licensing fees are payable one week before the opening performance of the play to Samuel French, Inc., at 45 W. 25th Street, New York, NY 10010.

Licensing fee of the required amount must be paid whether the play is presented for charity or gain and whether or not admission is charged.

Professional/Stock licensing fees quoted upon application to Samuel French, Inc.

For all other rights than those stipulated above, apply to: Samuel French, Inc., at 45 W. 25th Street, New York, NY 10010.

Particular emphasis is laid on the question of amateur or professional readings, permission and terms for which must be secured in writing from Samuel French, Inc.

Copying from this book in whole or in part is strictly forbidden by law, and the right of performance is not transferable.

Whenever the play is produced the following notice must appear on all programs, printing and advertising for the play: "Produced by special arrangement with Samuel French, Inc."

Due authorship credit must be given on all programs, printing and advertising for the play.

ISBN 978-0-573-69638-1   Printed in U.S.A.   #29047

No one shall commit or authorize any act or omission by which the copyright of, or the right to copyright, this play may be impaired.

No one shall make any changes in this play for the purpose of production.

Publication of this play does not imply availability for performance. Both amateurs and professionals considering a production are strongly advised in their own interests to apply to Samuel French, Inc., for written permission before starting rehearsals, advertising, or booking a theatre.

No part of this book may be reproduced, stored in a retrieval system, or transmitted in any form, by any means, now known or yet to be invented, including mechanical, electronic, photocopying, recording, videotaping, or otherwise, without the prior written permission of the publisher.

MUSIC USE NOTE

Licensees are solely responsible for obtaining formal written permission from copyright owners to use copyrighted music in the performance of this play and are strongly cautioned to do so. If no such permission is obtained by the licensee, then the licensee must use only original music that the licensee owns and controls. Licensees are solely responsible and liable for all music clearances and shall indemnify the copyright owners of the play and their licensing agent, Samuel French, Inc., against any costs, expenses, losses and liabilities arising from the use of music by licensees.

IMPORTANT BILLING AND CREDIT REQUIREMENTS

All producers of *WIDDERSHINS* must give credit to the Author of the Play in all programs distributed in connection with performances of the Play, and in all instances in which the title of the Play appears for the purposes of advertising, publicizing or otherwise exploiting the Play and/or a production. The name of the Author *must* appear on a separate line on which no other name appears, immediately following the title and *must* appear in size of type not less than fifty percent of the size of the title type.

In addition the following credit *must* be given in all programs and publicity information distributed in association with this piece:

Widdershins was presented as part of the First International Mystery Writer's Festival at RiverPark Center, Owensboro, Kentucky.

WIDDERSHINS was selected for the First International Mystery Writers Festival and had its first professional production at RiverPark Center, Owensboro, Kentucky, in June 2007. The play was directed by Wes Bartlett with the following cast:

MCGONIGLE	George Fleming
RUFFING	Grey Hurt
JENNY	Krystal Kimbley
ENGLISH	Donald Maley
NED	Aaron Brown
ANN	Amy Attaway
MRS ENGLISH	Debra Babich
FELICITY	Sara Jane Behl
CONSTANCE	Leslie Stovall
OLD BETTY	Lynda Turner

WIDDERSHINS was first produced October 13-22, 2006 at Pellissippi State College in Knoxville, Tennessee under the direction of Charles R. Miller with the following cast and creative team:

MCGONIGLE	Glen Ellington
RUFFING	Robby Griffith
JENNY	Kathryn Hale
ENGLISH	Kevin Velasco
NED	Andy Riggs
ANN	Dani Scott
MRS ENGLISH	Bonnie Blalock
FELICITY	Leslie Smith
CONSTANCE	Caroline Blasius
OLD BETTY	Lisa Garcia

Production Stage Manager/Costumes: Lesley Irminger
Stage Manager: Brittany Hodge
Assistant Stage Manager: Rebecca Scheidler
Lighting Designer: Leigh Brown
Set Designer: Brian Prather

CHARACTERS

MCGONIGLE
RUFFING
JENNY
ENGLISH
NED
ANN
MRS ENGLISH
FELICITY
CONSTANCE
OLD BETTY

SETTING

An old house near the Welsh border in the autumn of the year 1902. A desk with leather chair. A sofa. Books on shelves. A table with a chessboard, game in progress. A liquor cabinet with bottles and glasses. Down left is the door to the outside. Up left center, in one angle of a wall, a dark old mirror in a carved wooden frame, facing towards the desk, so the audience can't quite see into it. Upstage, an arch leading to the rest of the house. There is a rug in front of the sofa, and downstage, not visible to us, is the fireplace the sofa faces. The set should be open enough so that those characters who at certain points in the play seem to appear as dreams, hallucinations and/or memories may enter and exit at will, with maximum efficiency and minimum fuss.

The playwright wishes to thank the following for significant help and encouragement along the way: Lawrence Harbison, Zev Buffman, and Joseph Nigro.

ACT ONE

(We hear the voice of **MCGONIGLE** *as he opens the outer door, and moonlight streams into the room.* **MCGONIGLE** *and* **RUFFING** *enter, and* **MCGONIGLE** *lights a lamp as he speaks.)*

MCGONIGLE. I can make no sense of it whatsoever. They simply vanished. A man, his wife, and two daughters. Supper on the table. A fire in the fireplace. A chess game half played. No signs of violence or struggle. We've searched the place from one end to the other, combed the surrounding area. There's no evidence of any sort. I'm absolutely baffled. And it occurred to me that this was just your sort of thing.

RUFFING. Meaning what?

MCGONIGLE. Well, you know.

RUFFING. No, I don't.

MCGONIGLE. Yes, you do. Ninety-eight percent of the time, I'm as good or better than you at what we do. Procedure. Orderly investigation. But there's that odd two percent, falling within the range of the decidedly bizarre, which seems to be your particular territory. You've a kind of genius for what looks absurd and more or less hopeless.

RUFFING. I believe I'm flattered, Mac.

MCGONIGLE. You should be. Although I must confess you're a damned nuisance most of the rest of the time.

RUFFING. There's no evidence that anything at all unusual has happened, except that one evening a little before supper four people apparently vanished off the face of the earth.

MCGONIGLE. That's it. Everything left in place. Nothing odd at all, except perhaps for this.

*(He goes to the desk and gets a piece of paper, which he hands to **RUFFING**.)*

MCGONIGLE. *(cont.)* We found this on the desk, with just that one word written on it.

RUFFING. *(looking at the paper)* Widdershins.

MCGONIGLE. Widdershins. That's the one odd thing. Although probably it's nothing.

RUFFING. Widdershins. Well, that is somewhat odd, isn't it? Sounds vaguely familiar.

MCGONIGLE. My old granny said withershins. Wither, instead of widder. It's a country people's word. Quite ancient, I believe. Means against the sun, in the opposite direction of the way the sun goes. Backwards.

RUFFING. Counterclockwise.

MCGONIGLE. Yes, but the word's older than clocks, I'm sure.

RUFFING. That rings some sort of bell in my head, but I can't think what.

MCGONIGLE. The missing are James English, writer, forties, wife Eleanor, thirties, and two daughters, Constance and Felicity, in their late teens. Quiet people, lived here several years, no hint of trouble we can find. The husband seems to have painted a bit, hunted rabbits, read quite a lot, as you can see. Devoted wife. Her family seems to have money. The daughters are very bright, and rather beautiful. Here's a picture.

*(gets a photograph off the desk, shows **RUFFING**)*

Quite a handsome family altogether.

RUFFING. No witnesses?

MCGONIGLE. A girl who helps with chores and cooking, lives with her people on a farm down the lane, was the last, apparently, to see them. Went out for something, came back, found them gone, told her father, who called the authorities. There's a third daughter away at art school. She's come back now.

RUFFING. Where is the servant girl?

MCGONIGLE. *(sticking his head out the door)* Ned, send in Jenny, will you please?

(to **RUFFING***:)*

Very pretty lass. Lame, though. Shame about that.

JENNY. *(entering)* Yes sir?

MCGONIGLE. Inspector Ruffing here would like to ask you a few questions.

JENNY. I've already answered every question in the universe. I want to go home now.

RUFFING. I won't keep you long, Jenny, I promise. Just tell me what you found here.

JENNY. I found just what you see. Mrs English sent me to my father's to get some milk for supper. When I came back, they were gone.

RUFFING. What did you think, when you found them gone?

JENNY. I didn't know what to think. I looked around for them, but they were nowhere to be found. I did wonder for a moment if they might be playing some sort of joke on me. Felicity – the younger Miss English, could be – well, playful, on occasion.

RUFFING. Playful?

JENNY. That's not really the proper word. She – has an odd sense of humor. I suppose I half expected someone to jump out at me from behind the curtains. But I knew, of course, that the others would never have gone along with such foolishness. And yet I had this strange feeling that somebody was watching me. It was all so eerie. The clock ticking. The fire crackling in the fireplace. I thought perhaps I might be dreaming, so I tried to wake up, but I couldn't. Then I got very frightened and ran home.

RUFFING. Do you often dream of your employers, Jenny?

JENNY. What else have I got to dream about?

RUFFING. When you left to get the milk, there was nothing wrong here?

JENNY. No sir.

RUFFING. No argument, nothing troubling them?

JENNY. If there was, they said nothing to me about it.

RUFFING. Were Mr and Mrs English a happy couple, would you say?

JENNY. That was none of my business.

RUFFING. Does that mean no?

JENNY. They seemed happy enough. Who is happy? Nobody I know. May I go now?

RUFFING. You saw no one entering or leaving this place as you left or came back?

JENNY. No sir.

RUFFING. How long were you gone for the milk?

JENNY. I don't know. It wasn't very long. I don't walk as fast as some.

RUFFING. What exactly were they doing when you left?

JENNY. Mrs English and the girls were getting supper. Mr English was reading at his desk.

RUFFING. What was he reading?

JENNY. I don't know. A book.

RUFFING. Did you find any books on the desk, Mac?

MCGONIGLE. No. Just on the shelves.

RUFFING. What kind of book was it?

JENNY. I didn't notice.

RUFFING. What color was it? What size?

JENNY. I think it was a black book. An old one. He's always liked old books.

RUFFING. Do you see it here on the shelves?

JENNY. I don't know which it was, sir. He has so many. I just remember it was old and the pages were cream yellow and the cover was black. Why does that matter?

RUFFING. How were your relations with the English family?

JENNY. Relations?

RUFFING. Were you friendly with them?

JENNY. I'm their servant.

RUFFING. So they weren't friendly with you?

JENNY. They're friendly enough people. Mrs English is nice, but she's not familiar. The girls are very friendly sometimes but a bit moody. Constance is a thoughtful person. Felicity is more lively. They were decent to me. But I know my place, and they knew it, too.

RUFFING. And what about Mr English? Was he decent to you as well?

JENNY. Mr English was mostly occupied with his work.

RUFFING. Which was what?

JENNY. Which was writing.

RUFFING. Writing about what?

JENNY. Different things. Odd things.

RUFFING. What odd things? Odd in what sense?

JENNY. Superstitions. I don't know.

RUFFING. What kind of superstitions?

ENGLISH. *(Entering from another part of the house.* **RUFFING** *and* **MCGONIGLE** *remain, watching, as if listening to Jenny relate what we see played before us.)* There you are, Jenny. I want to ask you something.

JENNY. Yes, sir?

ENGLISH. You've lived here all your life. Are there stories about this place?

JENNY. Stories?

ENGLISH. Is this house supposed to be haunted? Are there strange creatures lurking about this place in local legend?

JENNY. Only foolish tales, sir.

ENGLISH. Yes, that's what I'm interested in. Foolish tales. Tell me a foolish tale or two about this place.

JENNY. I really can't remember any, sir.

ENGLISH. Come on, Jenny. Don't be shy. You can be a great help to me in my work.

JENNY. In your work?

ENGLISH. Yes, my work in foolish tales. I am a great believer in foolish tales, Jenny. I believe there is much truth locked in the deepest heart of foolishness. So tell me, are we haunted, or aren't we?

JENNY. Well, there are stories about – something being here.

ENGLISH. Really? What? A ghost?

JENNY. Not exactly, no.

ENGLISH. Something in this house?

JENNY. Not exactly in the house, no, sir. I don't remember much about it. You might want to ask Old Betty, from down the lane. She knows all the old stories, and a few I believe she's made up herself.

ENGLISH. And have you ever seen this thing, Jenny? This thing which is not exactly a ghost, and not exactly in the house?

JENNY. No, sir.

ENGLISH. You don't say that with much conviction.

JENNY. There are times when I have felt just a bit uncomfortable here, sir.

ENGLISH. Uncomfortable in what respect?

JENNY. Uneasy. As if –

ENGLISH. As if something were watching you?

JENNY. Are you mocking me, sir?

ENGLISH. I would never mock you, Jenny.

JENNY. I think you are.

ENGLISH. I'll tell you what. In the future, if I intend to mock you, I'll be sure to let you know first, all right?

(She looks at him uncertainly. He smiles at her, takes out a small leather bound notebook, sits down at the desk, and writes in it through what follows.)

RUFFING. So you believe Mr English was writing about superstitions connected with this house?

JENNY. I don't know, sir. I'm very tired, and I don't see why it matters what he was writing.

RUFFING. It's not your job to see, is it?

JENNY. I don't seem to have a job, now, do I? My job seems to have vanished, along with most of the people in my life, and I'm falling asleep on my feet, and I'm thoroughly sick of talking to policemen.

RUFFING. Yes, well, frankly, Jenny, so am I. All right. You can go now.

JENNY. Thank God.

(She starts to go.)

RUFFING. Jenny?

JENNY. What?

RUFFING. What do you think happened to them?

JENNY. How would I know?

RUFFING. You can't even guess?

JENNY. No. I can't guess.

RUFFING. I hope you have no bad dreams tonight, Jenny.

JENNY. *(looks at him for a moment, then:)* Same to you, sir.

(She turns and goes.)

RUFFING. She's lying.

MCGONIGLE. I don't see that. Seems like a nice enough girl to me. Bit of spirit there.

RUFFING. Fancy her, do you, McGonigle?

MCGONIGLE. No, I just – no.

RUFFING. Perhaps she is a nice girl, but I'll bet you my pension she's hiding something. Is there anything to drink around here?

MCGONIGLE. Over there, but you don't want to drink that.

RUFFING. Why don't I?

MCGONIGLE. For all we know, it could be poisoned. We were going to try it on the cat, but I got rather attached to the fellow.

RUFFING. Well, I'll be the cat, then. You're getting soft, Mac.

(He pours himself a drink.)

RUFFING. *(cont.)* What's wrong? You disapprove of drinking on duty? As I recall, you've been known to have a spot or two yourself.

MCGONIGLE. This is true.

RUFFING. Well, then. Down the hatch and call me Albert.

(He drinks.)

Ah. Damn good stuff. If it's poison, this is the way I want to go. Sure you don't want some?

MCGONIGLE. Don't think I'd better, thanks.

RUFFING. Suit yourself. I should go into a gagging fit and collapse now, just to alarm you, but I don't think I'm up to it at the moment.

(He pours himself another.)

MCGONIGLE. Are you all right, Johnny?

RUFFING. Of course I'm all right. Why wouldn't I be all right?

(He drinks.)

MCGONIGLE. You look a bit haggard.

RUFFING. Haggard? You think I look haggard?

MCGONIGLE. Somewhat, yes.

RUFFING. And what's your diagnosis, Mac? Why do you think I look haggard? Could it be that I haven't had two consecutive hours of sleep in the last six months? Why did you have me brought in on this?

MCGONIGLE. I told you. I thought it was your sort of puzzle.

RUFFING. Weren't feeling a bit sorry for me, were you?

MCGONIGLE. Certainly not.

RUFFING. Heard rumors, have you? Old Ruffing's hitting the bottle rather hard these days? Old Ruffing's falling apart since the wife died? Poor old Johnny's cracking up? John's off his noggin? Those rumors?

MCGONIGLE. I called you in because you're the best.

RUFFING. If you think that, you're the only one.

MCGONIGLE. No I'm not.

RUFFING. Our superiors certainly wouldn't agree with you.

MCGONIGLE. Our superiors can kiss my arse.

(*Pause.* **RUFFING** *looks at him, smiles.*)

RUFFING. Any suspicious characters seen lurking around these parts lately? I mean besides you and me.

MCGONIGLE. Strangers here are news very quickly. A stray tramp was through last week. We're tracking him down. And a rather bizarre person lives down the road in a tumbledown stone house. Insane, but harmless, I think. Beyond that, nothing.

(*pause*)

She was a wonderful woman, your wife.

RUFFING. Yes.

MCGONIGLE. I fancied her myself, actually.

RUFFING. Did you?

MCGONIGLE. And your daughter's just the image of her. Smart as a whip, too.

RUFFING. Yes. She is.

MCGONIGLE. Nothing for it but to do the work, yes? Continue the investigation.

(*Pause.* **RUFFING** *looks at him.* **NED** *enters.*)

NED. Excuse me sir. The other daughter's here.

MCGONIGLE. Good. Bring her in, will you, Ned?

NED. Yes sir. This way, please, miss.

(*He holds the door open as* **ANN** *enters.*)

MCGONIGLE. Hello, Miss English, I'm Inspector McGonigle. I'm sorry to –

ANN. It's not English, Inspector. My name is Ann Howard. I'm not actually their daughter. Mrs English was a close friend of my mother, and when my parents died, they took me in. You still don't know what's become of them?

MCGONIGLE. We're working on it. I've brought Inspector Ruffing here in to help.

ANN. Is this how he helps, by drinking up all the liquor in the house?

MCGONIGLE. It's all part of the investigation, miss.

RUFFING. How long have you been with the English family?

ANN. Seven years. Since I was fourteen.

RUFFING. And you have no idea where they might have gone?

ANN. I really can't imagine. They wouldn't have just left like that.

RUFFING. Were Mr and Mrs English good to you?

ANN. They were very good to me. Why are we speaking in the past tense? Do you believe they're dead?

RUFFING. Do you?

ANN. How am I supposed to know?

RUFFING. Did they have enemies that you know of? Anyone who might want to do them harm?

ANN. No. Absolutely not.

RUFFING. Do you know what Mr English was working on?

ANN. Working on?

RUFFING. Writing. What was Mr English writing?

ANN. His first book was on the Impressionists. But then he got interested in other things – folklore, superstition, Druids. I don't know what all else.

RUFFING. Druids?

ANN. Yes.

RUFFING. Forgive me, but I'm having a little trouble seeing the connection between the Impressionists and the Druids.

ANN. His mind often made unusual connections. I believe that's a characteristic of genuinely creative people.

RUFFING. So you found Mr English to be particularly – creative?

ANN. He was – he is – a rather unusual individual. Almost – mystical.

RUFFING. Mystical. Do you mean he was insane?

ANN. Do you think all mystics are insane, Inspector?

RUFFING. I imagine it doesn't hurt any. The ability to make unusual connections is also, I believe, a characteristic of lunatics. And, now and then, police inspectors. Do you know where he kept his manuscripts?

ANN. I would expect on his desk.

RUFFING. All we found there was this piece of paper.

(He hands her the paper.)

ANN. Widdershins. That's very odd.

RUFFING. *(watching her carefully)* Do you know what it means?

ANN. *(meeting his eyes, then looking away before she answers)* It's some sort of ballad or fairy tale word, isn't it? Burd Ellen went widdershins round the church.

RUFFING. Childe Rowland to the dark tower came.

ANN. Yes, that's it. Burd Ellen goes widdershins – counter-clockwise, the wrong way, round the church in search of something, I forget what, perhaps a red ball, and then –

RUFFING. And then she vanishes.

ANN. Yes. She vanishes. Wait. Here it is.

(She gets a book down from the shelves.)

Joseph Jacobs. *English Fairy Tales.* It was a favorite of the girls when they were small. Mr English read it to them.

RUFFING. My wife read that to my daughter. Odd. Do you know why anyone would write this word on a sheet of paper and leave it on the desk?

ANN. No. I have no idea.

RUFFING. Was there trouble in this house? Arguments, tension?

ANN. There might have been small tensions now and then, but I wouldn't say there was any significant trouble.

RUFFING. But when these small tensions did occur, what was the cause?

ANN. Mr English didn't like being bothered in his work. That could be a small source of tension, on occasion.

MRS ENGLISH. *(Entering from within the house.* **RUFFING** *and* **MCGONIGLE** *remain and watch, as before.)* James, the pipe is leaking again.

ENGLISH. *(absorbed in his work at the desk)* Just a moment.

MRS ENGLISH. The pipe won't wait a moment. I've tried reasoning with it. James, there is water on the kitchen floor.

ENGLISH. Well, mop it up, why don't you? Just let me finish this thought.

MRS ENGLISH. You never finish a thought, you just keep going on from one thing to the next. If I wait for you to finish a thought, we'll need an ark.

ENGLISH. Do you consider it your function on earth to keep jabbering at me until you drive whatever is in my head clean out of it?

MRS ENGLISH. Don't talk to me that way.

ANN. I'll take a look at it.

MRS ENGLISH. Don't be silly. It's his job.

ANN. Why is it his job?

MRS ENGLISH. He's the man. When things get wet, it's his responsibility.

ANN. I've as much likelihood of fixing a pipe as he does.

MRS ENGLISH. An orangutan has as much likelihood as he does. That's not the point.

ANN. Then what is the point?

ENGLISH. The point is, will you bloody women please stop yapping for three minutes so I can get this down before it pops right out of my head?

MRS ENGLISH. Oh, rubbish. You can write just as well after you fix the pipe as before it, only I won't be stomping about knee deep in a swamp.

ENGLISH. WILL YOU SHUT UP? WOMAN, YOU ARE A WALKING DAMNED PROVOCATION FOR BLOODY MURDER.

MRS ENGLISH. If you're going to murder me, please fix the pipe first, I don't want my corpse lying around in three feet of water.

ENGLISH. That's it. It's gone. I have no idea what I was going to write.

MRS ENGLISH. Then it couldn't have been all that important, could it?

ENGLISH. *(holding his head in frustration)* Ahhhhhhhhh!

MRS ENGLISH. Don't growl, dear. You'll frighten the cat.

ENGLISH. *(to* **ANN***)* I'm going in the kitchen to drown myself.

(He disappears into the house.)

MRS ENGLISH. Take my advice, Annie. Marry a man who knows what to do when you've sprung a leak.

(She follows him into the kitchen.)

RUFFING. A walking provocation for bloody murder.

ANN. It was just a figure of speech. I hope you're not thinking Mr English might have harmed his family.

RUFFING. When was the last time you heard from them?

ANN. I had a note from Felicity just the other day, and she seemed fine.

RUFFING. Well, something wasn't fine. One moment four people are in their house, preparing to sit down to supper, and a few minutes later they've all vanished. Something was clearly very wrong somewhere. May I see the note she sent you?

ANN. I don't have it with me.

RUFFING. Can you remember what it said?

ANN. I really don't think that's relevant.

RUFFING. Why don't you let me decide that?

ANN. You wouldn't understand it.

RUFFING. Why wouldn't I?

ANN. Because Felicity had – has – a rather odd sense of humor. You would have to know her, to be brought up with her, to have any real sense of what she was communicating.

RUFFING. Just tell me what the note said.

ANN. It said, "When I have done talking with the Eldest Magician, I will walk into the big Miz-Maze, because I have to."

RUFFING. What in God's name is that supposed to mean?

ANN. It's a quote from Rudyard Kipling.

RUFFING. That does not enlighten me a great deal. What did she mean by it?

ANN. I don't know. She's always been fond of puzzles and enigmas.

RUFFING. But you must have taken it to mean something. Surely you were not in the habit of receiving completely nonsensical messages from her.

ANN. She was fond of nonsense. She found it meaningful.

RUFFING. Who is the Eldest Magician?

ANN. I expect she was referring to her father.

RUFFING. Her father was a magician?

ANN. He was interested in arcane subjects.

RUFFING. And what is the big Miz-Maze?

ANN. A maze, a labyrinth. It was a kind of metaphor, perhaps, for her confusion.

MCGONIGLE. Well, she does sound confused. I know I'm confused.

RUFFING. What was she confused about?

ANN. Felicity is a rather gifted person. And I know it's been very lonely for her at times, growing up out here.

FELICITY. *(Appearing from within the house.* **RUFFING** *and* **MCGONIGLE** *stay and observe, as before.)* Oh, God, Annie, don't leave me. I'll go insane here without you.

ANN. Felicity, if I'm going to be an artist, I must go to art school.

FELICITY. But great artists don't go to school. Did Hieronymus Bosch go to school?

ANN. Well, not any school I'd want to go to, but I'm sure he must have studied with somebody or other, however demented they might have been, and so must I.

FELICITY. Then take me with you.

ANN. I can't take you with me.

FELICITY. Yes you can. Hide me in your luggage. Stuff me in your trunk.

ANN. I'm not stuffing you in my trunk.

FELICITY. If I'm discovered, I'll pretend I'm a ventriloquist's dummy.

ANN. Now you're being silly.

FELICITY. I'm not being silly, I'm going berserk. I mean it. I shall go mad. The only entertainment I get is going out to the barn to shoot rats. There is no one else to talk to here.

ANN. Of course there is. Talk to Constance.

FELICITY. Constance doesn't talk. She broods.

ANN. Talk to your mother, then.

FELICITY. Very funny.

ANN. Well, then talk to Father.

FELICITY. I can't talk to him any more. He's so strange lately.

ANN. He's just preoccupied with his work.

FELICITY. Yes, that's what frightens me. Ann, I'm quite serious, you know. I wonder sometimes if I'm not already a bit insane.

ANN. You're not insane. You're unusual, but you're not insane.

FELICITY. Father's insane.

ANN. No he's not.

FELICITY. Yes, I think he is. Do you know he's been seeing things?

ANN. What things?

FELICITY. I don't know what it is, exactly, but I've caught him suddenly dashing to the window to stick his head out, or looking over his shoulder as if he's trying to catch somebody sneaking up on him, or bolting outside and running around the house, looking for God knows what.

ANN. Are you sure it's not you who's been seeing things?

FELICITY. Well, if it is, that proves my point, doesn't it? Clearly I'm going insane here. So you really must take me with you, to save my sanity.

ANN. You can't go with me. But I promise to write to you every week, and to come home and see you as often as I can.

FELICITY. You're lucky, you know, to be getting out now, before it happens.

ANN. Before what happens?

FELICITY. Something's going to happen. Soon, I think.

ANN. What are you talking about?

FELICITY. Nothing. Don't mind me. I'm only a ventriloquist's dummy. Think of me when you open up your trunk.

(They look at each other. **FELICITY** *kisses her on the cheek and goes to sit on the couch.)*

RUFFING. What did she think was going to happen?

ANN. I don't know. She was just upset at my leaving.

RUFFING. But she said her father's preoccupation with his work frightened her. Why would it frighten her?

ANN. Look, I'm certain this has nothing to do with anything. Why aren't you out looking for them, instead of asking me stupid questions about Felicity and Rudyard Kipling?

MCGONIGLE. We have people looking for them.

ANN. Well, they're doing a pretty rotten job of it, aren't they?

RUFFING. I see you have a temper, Miss Howard.

ANN. And I see you have a drinking problem, Inspector Ruffing.

RUFFING. Be that as it may, I'm all you've got here, and I'm trying to help you. The truth is, we don't know what's important at this point. What may seem foolish or irrelevant to you might in fact be of great significance, and I need to understand who these people were, and what was going on in this house before they disappeared. Then perhaps we can find out what's become of them. Do you understand that?

ANN. No. I don't understand anything about this.

RUFFING. Was Mr English really behaving in the odd way Felicity described? Was he looking over his shoulder, peering out the window, and running around the house?

ANN. It was just – there were things going on in his head.

RUFFING. So you did see him do those things?

ANN. Yes, I suppose so, only it wasn't –

RUFFING. Which direction did he run?

ANN. Which direction?

RUFFING. Yes. Which direction did he run around the house? Was it clockwise, or counterclockwise?

ANN. I suppose it was – counterclockwise.

RUFFING. Widdershins.

ANN. Yes. Widdershins.

FELICITY. Widdershins.

ANN. But you don't think –

RUFFING. The girl goes widdershins round the church and then she vanishes.

FELICITY. And then she vanishes.

RUFFING. Tell me about his work. What was it that frightened his daughter so much?

ANN. I don't know.

RUFFING. Come on, why the Impressionists? Why Druids? What was the connection?

ANN. His interest in the Impressionists seemed to revolve around the perception of reality as blurred, indistinct, ambiguous as to boundaries. He was interested in the act of perception, and its relationship to truth. He also wrote about labyrinths and time. His real interest, I think, was the nature of reality itself, the fundamental nature of human experience, conscious and otherwise.

ENGLISH. *(appearing again from within the house)* I think perhaps it was my wretched eyesight that first attracted me to the Impressionists. They were the painters who seemed to most accurately describe the world as it appeared to me. I take off my spectacles and the world becomes a Renoir, a Sisley, and I realize that to see things very clearly is only to see the illusion more clearly, the illusion that the world is solid and has fixed boundaries.

*(***CONSTANCE** *appears upstage, listening.)*

But when the spectacles are off and the world seems to flicker like candlelight and you can feel the fog of dreams about your ears, you know that the world is in fact a shimmering labyrinth of color and ambiguity, irony and complexity, the boundaries all blurred. All boundaries are illusions or half truths, directly related to the limitations of the perceiver.

CONSTANCE. Has it ever occurred to you, Felicity, that our Papa might be stark, raving mad?

FELICITY. No. It never has.

ENGLISH. Renoir's hands, you know, were like claws in the end, he had to have the brushes strapped to them because he couldn't hold them any more, and still he painted, and the painting was joy, because in the act of painting he felt closer to the truth than anywhere else in his life. All is the association of blurred images. God swims in ambiguous soup. We are all the product of primeval soup, and we live at the bottom of an ocean of it. Radiation, light, particles we can't see, can't hold onto, can't grasp, like God, the Behemoth in the soup.

CONSTANCE. Childe Rowland to the dark tower came.

FELICITY. Widdershins.

ENGLISH. Light unifies all things. God is the exchange of colored reflections. I believe in the pathetic fallacy. Or rather, that a belief in any sort of diety is the real pathetic fallacy, but the feeling that nature is somehow connected to human emotions, while an obvious lie, is also true if you come at it from the other way round, that since we are a part of the natural world, human emotions tend to be reflected powerfully in natural events, all things being connected to all other things. Without light there is no creation, all is chaos. Light is the beginning of order. In the act of composition, that which is hidden in the dark inside us enters deeply into the dark private parts of the nature of things in a sexual conjunction, and light is seen, as the sparrow flying through the brightly lit hall at night, a passage from dark to light to dark. And thus have I travelled in my studies, from the contemplation of light, to the serious study of darkness.

CONSTANCE. Hell is murky.

FELICITY. So is he.

RUFFING. From light to darkness, hence, the Druids? They were the darkness of which he spoke? The dark to which he turned his studies? He had looked for God in the light, and, failing to find him there, he looked then into the darkness.

ANN. I suppose that's possible. I don't know. That is about the time I left for art school.

RUFFING. Art school must be rather expensive. Was Mr English paying for your education?

ANN. Yes.

RUFFING. He must have been very fond of you, I mean, considering that you were not actually his daughter.

ANN. Well, neither, for that matter, were the others. Constance and Felicity were the daughters of Mrs English by a previous marriage, so they were no more the actual children of Mr English than I am.

RUFFING. Ah. Now, that's interesting.

CONSTANCE. No it's not.

RUFFING. What do you know about the first husband?

ANN. Very little. He was a ship's surgeon, lost at sea when the girls were quite small.

RUFFING. His body was not recovered?

ANN. No. I don't believe so.

RUFFING. Do you know what kind of man he was?

ANN. Rather harsh, I gathered. The girls had only a few memories of him. He was away so much, and it was a long time ago to them. But Mrs English seemed – well, once we had a conversation about the brutality of men in general, and how lucky she felt to have found Mr English.

*(**MRS ENGLISH** appears, comes over to sit on the sofa.)*

I gathered from this that she had not had an altogether easy time of it with her first husband.

MRS ENGLISH. I wish you were a happier girl, Ann.

*(**RUFFING, MCGONIGLE, ENGLISH, FELICITY** and **CONSTANCE** all remain, watching what follows.)*

ANN. I'm happy enough, thank you.

MRS ENGLISH. You don't seem so to me. You need to find a nice man.

ANN. I don't think finding a nice man is necessarily going to be the solution to all my troubles. Or, for that matter, any of my troubles.

MRS ENGLISH. Listen to me. I've had a cruel husband and I've had a kind one. Believe me, it makes a world of difference as to how you see the world. Do not take a decent man for granted. That is a great mistake many girls make.

ANN. I take nothing for granted. I'm an orphan.

MRS ENGLISH. I just think that if you met a nice young man –

ANN. There are no nice young men, there are only degrees of bestiality.

MRS ENGLISH. What on earth do you mean by that?

ANN. Nothing.

MRS ENGLISH. Well, now, you must mean something by it. Everything means something.

ANN. Does it?

MRS ENGLISH. I think it does.

ANN. Well, you're wrong.

CONSTANCE. Annie's upset.

FELICITY. And we know why, don't we?

RUFFING. What has caused you to be so cynical about men?

ANN. Any woman with half a brain is cynical about men.

RUFFING. What about Felicity and Constance? How did they feel about men?

ANN. They hardly knew any but Mr English.

RUFFING. And?

ANN. And they adored him.

RUFFING. And did you adore him?

FELICITY. Mustn't lie, now, Annie.

ANN. We got along well enough.

ENGLISH. Ann. Come here. I want to show you something.

RUFFING. You didn't like him.

ENGLISH. Ann?

CONSTANCE. Careful how you answer. Men are here to trick us.

FELICITY. All questions are trick questions.

ANN. I liked him very much. And I was grateful to him. For taking me in.

RUFFING. Then what was wrong between you and Mr English?

ANN. Nothing was wrong.

RUFFING. I don't believe that's true.

ANN. Are you calling me a liar?

OLD BETTY. *(A strange looking old hermit, bursting abruptly in from outside.)* Well, ballocks and pig's piss, the bloody place is crawling with gargoyles.

MCGONIGLE. I beg your pardon?

OLD BETTY. You'd better, with a face like that. Who the hell are you?

MCGONIGLE. Who the hell am I? Who the hell are you?

OLD BETTY. I know who I am. And watch your language in front of the lady.

ANN. Hello, Betty.

NED. *(trailing in guiltily after her)* I'm sorry, sir. I don't know how she got past me.

OLD BETTY. I clouded his mind.

ANN. It's all right, it's just Betty.

RUFFING. Betty who?

OLD BETTY. Old Betty who lives down the lane. I heard what happened.

RUFFING. What did you hear?

OLD BETTY. Whispering in my head. Old Betty listens at the fire. This has always been a dark place.

RUFFING. You mean this house?

OLD BETTY. This house and long before.

RUFFING. Who is this person?

ANN. Betty is the local, well, seer, of sorts. She sells herbs from her garden, and reads palms and such. Charms warts. Finds water.

MCGONIGLE. From the tumbledown stone house. I'll get rid of her. Come along, Betty.

OLD BETTY. Hands off, churl. Unclean. Unclean.

RUFFING. No, let her stay a moment. Tell me, Betty, why is this a dark place?

OLD BETTY. It's never a good thing to build in one of their places.

RUFFING. Whose places?

OLD BETTY. The old people. The dark people. The others. The lost ones.

RUFFING. I see.

OLD BETTY. No you don't. You don't see nothing yet. But you will. More than you want to.

RUFFING. Why was it not good to build here?

OLD BETTY. Because it's theirs. From the old time. Sacred places. They come up and get you.

MCGONIGLE. Up from where?

OLD BETTY. Up from below, you clotpole. Where else would they come up from?

MCGONIGLE. We've searched the basement. There's nobody there.

OLD BETTY. I'm not talking about no basement.

MCGONIGLE. Then what are you talking about?

OLD BETTY. Spend a night here, and you'll find out. Just like they did. This room is full of dead people.

RUFFING. What do you know about what happened here?

MCGONIGLE. She doesn't know anything. She's insane.

OLD BETTY. I know if you enter a fairy dwelling, you must stick a fish hook in the door, so the good people can't shut you in forever. They don't like iron, you see. They come from way before that. To keep a deer carcass from them, stick a knife in it. A lost child is one the fairies take. And if you meet any in the land of faerie, you must cut off their heads, no matter how pleasing to you they may appear. I know that much.

RUFFING. Uh huh. Well, thank you very much, Betty, for those insights, and if we have any more questions for you, that nice young man there whose mind you clouded will come and escort you here again, all right?

OLD BETTY. He's trying to kill me, too, you know.

RUFFING. Who is?

OLD BETTY. The dark one. Old Nick. I am followed everywhere I go by chickens. The chickens know me as a hen wife and wart charmer, and they pay me due respect to my face, but they plot behind my back. They work for him. The chickens plot to murder me because I have eaten their children.

MCGONIGLE. Yes, well, come along, Betty, Ned will protect you from the chickens, won't you, Neddy?

OLD BETTY. *(as* **NED** *and* **MCGONIGLE** *are ushering her out)* To find them you must go three times widdershins.

RUFFING. Wait a minute. What did you say?

OLD BETTY. When? Who?

RUFFING. Three times what?

OLD BETTY. Widdershins. Go three times widdershins, and each time say, open, door, open, door, and the third time, the door will open.

MCGONIGLE. Widdershins?

OLD BETTY. Yes. Are ye deaf, mooncalf? It must be widdershins. The right way round won't work.

RUFFING. Where did you get that word, widdershins?

OLD BETTY. Where did I get it?

RUFFING. Yes. Why did you happen to say that word? What put it in your head?

OLD BETTY. It is the dark one, up to his foul, naked deeds. Be him alive or be him dead, dash his brains out from his head.

RUFFING. Betty, do you know what happened here?

OLD BETTY. Do you?

RUFFING. No. I'm trying to find out.

OLD BETTY. Yes, well, that's dangerous, ain't it? So did he, and look where it got him. Straight to hell.

RUFFING. Do you mean Mr English?

OLD BETTY. I don't know what I mean. All these dead people here are making me tired. Old Betty needs to rest.

RUFFING. *(showing her the piece of paper)* Do you know anything about this?

OLD BETTY. *(looking not at the paper but at* **RUFFING***)* I know the man in the moon's a cannibal. And I know you're grieving.

RUFFING. Am I?

OLD BETTY. A pretty woman died. You have her picture in a ticking thing. You loved her too much. We pay for that. Never give all the heart. Save part for yourself. Otherwise, you're eaten up and lost.

(Pause. **RUFFING** *looks at her.)*

RUFFING. What happened to these people, Betty? Where have they gone?

OLD BETTY. They've gone where she went, the girl in your pocket, to the other place. And somebody here has death in their eyes. Sad, it is. But the saddest thing is a mad girl. I'm going home now.

(She starts out. To **MCGONIGLE***:)*

OLD BETTY. Get out of my way, clod, or I'll curse your nipples into giving blood.

RUFFING. It's all right, Mac. Let her go. Ned, see her home, would you?

NED. Yes, sir.

OLD BETTY. Yes, this one here's a pretty fellow, although he has a swollen left ballock. We can fix that. Come with me and take off your pants. And don't step on the chickens.

(She goes.)

NED. *(looking back at them nervously as he follows her)* Pray for me.

(They are gone.)

ANN. Inspector, are you all right?

RUFFING. I'm fine.

ANN. Your face is very pale. Did she say something that –

RUFFING. Will you be staying in town for the present, Miss Howard?

ANN. I'll be staying here. This is my home.

RUFFING. All right. We'll keep someone here with you, just in case.

ANN. In case what?

RUFFING. Do you mind if I stay here, in this room tonight? I'll be no trouble.

ANN. I doubt that very much. I need to get my things.

(She looks at him briefly, then goes out the door.)

MCGONIGLE. We can leave Ned to watch over her.

RUFFING. No. The answer is right here somewhere, in this house. I need to spend some time here to find out what it is.

MCGONIGLE. She's right, you know. You don't look well at all, Johnny.

RUFFING. How the devil do you suppose the old witch pulled that word out of the air like that?

MCGONIGLE. Sometimes mad people seem to read your mind, but it's just that they pick up stray bits of information and throw them out at odd times. Probably she saw that piece of paper on some other visit. It really supports the theory that it's been on his desk for some time and has nothing to do with this case.

RUFFING. But how did she know about my wife?

MCGONIGLE. She could see the grief in your face. Charlatans read people. It's a fortune teller's trick. John, if you're not feeling up to this –

RUFFING. I'm feeling up to any damned thing, so stop patronizing me.

MCGONIGLE. All right. Sorry. I'll just give Miss Howard a hand with her bags, then. It's great having you back, Johnny.

RUFFING. Yes.

(MCGONIGLE looks at him for a moment, then goes out. RUFFING pours himself another drink, sits, takes out a watch from his pocket, opens it, looks inside at a picture.)

How did she know you were in there? How did she know?

(He sits there, head in his hands. FELICITY comes over and touches his hair. He doesn't seem to notice.)

FELICITY. Inside us, we know. Inside us we know each one the time and means of our death, and the place. We have only to remember it, and it happens.

CONSTANCE. It happens and you remember it.

ENGLISH. The order in which things happen is one thing. The order in which they come to our knowledge is quite another. And the order in which we finally understand them – that is a different animal altogether.

FELICITY. One could almost pity the man.

CONSTANCE. No, I don't think so.

FELICITY. No, you're right, never pity a man. That is death to the soul. Pity is always death to the soul. You must go three times widdershins round the church to find the lost girl.

CONSTANCE. He has a dead woman in his watch.

FELICITY. He mourns in praise of nakedness and despair.

CONSTANCE. I smell the blood of a Christian man.

FELICITY. The ultimate destination is always sacrifice.

MRS ENGLISH. Everything means something.

ENGLISH. In much wisdom is much grief.

FELICITY. Widdershins.

CONSTANCE. Widdershins.

RUFFING. What does it mean? What does it mean?

ENGLISH. Do you play chess, Inspector?

RUFFING. Not well.

ENGLISH. The thing is, to have a puzzle with boundaries, yet a nearly infinite interior labyrinth in which to move about and investigate and become lost, that is somehow comforting. Both that the labyrinth is more or less infinite, but also that there are certain boundaries. That is, the way certain pieces must be moved. The border of the chessboard itself. People get very nervous when boundaries are crossed, don't you find that? They want a game with rules.

RUFFING. But what are the rules of this game?

ENGLISH. You know, Inspector, I believe you've had entirely too much to drink.

RUFFING. Where are your daughters? Where is your wife?

ENGLISH. Where is *your* daughter? Where is *your* wife?

RUFFING. This is not about my family.

ENGLISH. Are you certain? Because I think it is. I think that's exactly what this is about. You and I are in the same position, on God's chessboard. We are playing out the same game. We have both made the terrible miscalculation of loving mortal creatures, and we are both men who have devoted our lives to making investigations into truth. When you look in the mirror, I am what you see.

RUFFING. Are you here? Are you here, or am I dreaming you?

ENGLISH. A question I have often asked myself. And a question for which I have no satisfactory answer. I have spent much time walking the mountains of the moon, pondering this question.

RUFFING. I'm losing my mind.

ENGLISH. Quite possibly. The moon, you see, is much closer in this place. Do you know Hopkins? The mind has mountains, frightful, sheer, no-man fathomed.

RUFFING. I am. I'm imagining you.

ENGLISH. But am I also imagining you? The Druids believed that the world is in a constant state of flux, kept in motion by fire and water. They had a complex hierarchy of gods, but it was a secret who they were and how one was to deal with them. For the Druids, death was not the end. The soul transmigrates into new bodies. In the near presence of death, the Druids would sometimes be visited by the god in the form of a bird. A raven, perhaps?

RUFFING. I am having a nightmare. I must wake myself up.

ENGLISH. I thought you were looking for the truth.

RUFFING. I am looking for the truth.

ENGLISH. Then surely you must understand that sometimes, to find the truth, one must journey deeper and deeper into the nightmare.

RUFFING. What's happened to your family? What have you done with them?

FELICITY. We're right here, just over your shoulder, at the back of your head.

ENGLISH. Do you know Jephthah's daughter?

RUFFING. That's in the Old Testament, isn't it?

ENGLISH. Or, if you prefer the pagans, Agamemnon and Iphigenia. Look in the eyes of a murderer, and you will see a victim. But look in the eyes of the victim, and you will see the murderer. Look in the eyes of God, and you will see –

RUFFING. What? What will I see?

(The light begins to fade.)

What will I see when I look in the eyes of God?

CONSTANCE. You must look in the mirror for that.

RUFFING. The mirror?

(sound of a clock beginning to chime)

MRS ENGLISH. My dear, have you not forgot to wind up the clock?

(She disappears into the house.)

RUFFING. The clock? What about the clock?

ENGLISH. Pardon me. I must go wind up the wife's clock.

(He follows his wife into the house. The clock continues to chime. **ANN** *appears.)*

ANN. Inspector?

RUFFING. Yes? What? What about the clock?

ANN. It's just struck midnight. I'm sorry. I didn't mean to wake you.

RUFFING. Midnight?

ANN. I don't mind telling you, I feel very safe with you guarding me, Inspector.

RUFFING. It seems you've caught me sleeping on the job.

ANN. You looked as if you needed it. Don't worry. Ned is in the kitchen, eating everything in sight. Are you hungry?

RUFFING. I'm all right.

ANN. You should eat.

RUFFING. I've been having a rather extraordinarily vivid nightmare. All of this information rolling about in my head. The Impressionists attempted to paint exactly what they saw, even if they had rather bad eyesight. As if just looking deeply enough, even from within one's own limitations, one might somehow see to the core of things, the place where God presumably lives. But apparently seeing wasn't enough, things were hidden, just out windows, just at the back of his head, and so he moved on to the Druids. The idea that truth is somehow in hiding is the basis of all occult studies. That's what occult means – secret, hidden. If you can't see truth by looking directly at things, then you must try catching a glimpse of it out the corner of your eye, as it were, yes?

ANN. I suppose so.

RUFFING. Was he capable of violence?

ANN. Anyone is capable of violence.

RUFFING. Even you?

ANN. If sufficiently provoked.

RUFFING. And what would provoke you to violence, Miss Howard?

ANN. I expect very much the same sort of thing that would provoke you, Inspector. But you're going in the wrong direction with this. Mr English was simply not a violent person.

RUFFING. Tell that to the rabbits.

ANN. The rabbits?

RUFFING. Yes. Mac said he enjoyed shooting rabbits. If that isn't evidence of homicidal tendencies, I don't know what is.

ANN. Oh, certainly you can't think –

RUFFING. The gun. Where is the gun?

ANN. The gun?

RUFFING. Yes. The gun. His gun. He shot rabbits. Felicity shot rats in the barn. Where is the gun? Where did they keep the gun?

ANN. It always hung on the wall, right –

(She looks.)

It's gone. The gun is gone.

RUFFING. So wherever they went, they took a gun with them. Perhaps they've fallen down a rabbit hole.

ANN. I want you to know, Inspector, that if my family is not found soon, I'm going to report your unprofessional behavior to your superiors.

RUFFING. I'm afraid they already know.

ANN. Excuse me. I'm rather tired. I'm going to bed now. Do you want the light left on?

RUFFING. Yes, thank you.

(She turns the light off.)

ANN. Good night, Inspector.

(She goes. **RUFFING** *sits there, amid the eerie shadows of the firelight.)*

RUFFING. They took the gun. Where did they take the gun?

(He pours himself another drink. **FELICITY** *and* **CONSTANCE** *watch him.)*

FELICITY. He's drinking again.

CONSTANCE. This man is a mess.

FELICITY. You know what it is, don't you?

CONSTANCE. The dead wife. The lost daughter.

FELICITY. Well, that, yes. But it's more than that. It's the feeling. The feeling he has that somebody is looking over his shoulder. He can hear whispering, in the corners of the house. And he feels that somebody is lurking, just at the back of his head, don't you, Inspector?

RUFFING. Of course not.

CONSTANCE. Then who are you talking to, Johnny?

RUFFING. Nobody. I am talking to nobody. Or to myself. Which amounts to the same thing. As I am nobody. And nobody is me. And I hear no voices. And I do not, I absolutely do not, feel the nearly overwhelming conviction of the presence of something just over my shoulder, just at the back of my head, just out the window, just at the border of awareness. I do not feel the presence of this thing, and I am not going mad. Three times backwards round the church.

(He holds his glass up, as if making a toast.)

Widdershins.

FELICITY. Widdershins.

CONSTANCE. Three times round the church backwards.

RUFFING. What has happened here? What has happened here?

FELICITY. Once upon a time, there were two little girls.

CONSTANCE. And they took a long walk to a very dark place, with their father, and their mother.

FELICITY. Into the darkness.

CONSTANCE. Into the abyss.

FELICITY. And they never came back.

CONSTANCE. What I have seen of nakedness is ecstasy and terror.

FELICITY. Darkness. Old things. Old places. Dark places. A darkened mirror.

CONSTANCE. Jephthah's daughter. Iphigenia.

FELICITY. Lost places.

CONSTANCE. Where there is no light.

FELICITY. Three times round the church backwards.

CONSTANCE. Widdershins.

FELICITY. Widdershins.

RUFFING. Widdershins.

(He drinks. The girls watch him sadly. The light fades on them and goes out. Just the sound of the ticking clock in the darkness. End of Act One.)

ACT TWO

(Sound of the clock ticking in the darkness. Lights up to reveal **RUFFING** *alone, drink in his hand, staring into the old dark mirror on the upstage wall. The following evening. After a moment,* **MCGONIGLE** *enters.)*

MCGONIGLE. Inspector? Johnny?

RUFFING. Interesting mirror, isn't it? Quite old, I think. Strange carvings around it. What do you make of it, Mac?

MCGONIGLE. *(coming over to peer at it with* **RUFFING***)* Demons of some sort. As in castle spouting. Gargoyles.

RUFFING. We look rather like gargoyles ourselves, don't we? Grotesquely distorted images. At least, I hope it's the mirror.

MCGONIGLE. Jenny is here.

RUFFING. Yes. Well. I don't look forward to this. Best get it over with.

MCGONIGLE. We can do this tomorrow, if you're not feeling up to it.

RUFFING. How I'm feeling has nothing to do with anything. Bring her in.

MCGONIGLE. Want me to take the drink?

RUFFING. No, I'll hang onto it, thank you, Mac.

MCGONIGLE. I only thought –

RUFFING. Yes. I know what you thought.

MCGONIGLE. *(looks at him for a moment, then goes to the outer door and opens it)* Ned, bring her in now.

RUFFING. Don't worry, Mac. I'll be gentle, more or less.

JENNY. *(being ushered in by* **NED***)* I don't know why you people have to keep hauling me over here. I've got chores to do. Some people have to work, you know.

39

NED. I've heard rumors to that effect.

RUFFING. I promise not to keep you long, Jenny. We've actually had a rather busy day today, believe it or not, poking about in drawers and such, and I just wanted to ask you about something we found hidden away in the back of a closet.

JENNY. What's that?

RUFFING. Some very interesting paintings done by Mr English.

JENNY. Oh?

RUFFING. Nudes, actually. Nude studies of a very lovely young girl. A girl who looks remarkably like you.

JENNY. Does she?

RUFFING. Did you pose for Mr English?

JENNY. I'm not ashamed. He said there was nothing wrong in it. He said they do it all the time in France. I'm a good girl.

RUFFING. Did Mrs English know you modelled nude for her husband?

JENNY. I don't think so. We only did it when she was in town with the girls, or visiting friends. I don't expect she'd have liked it much. She was a bit more – conventional than Mr English. He wasn't like anybody else in the world. He saw things differently. He said that if you looked at things in a certain way, taught yourself to pay a kind of passionate attention, to look with different eyes, or at least different spectacles, you could see things other people couldn't see.

RUFFING. What kind of things?

JENNY. He said he was looking for God. But that other people had been looking in the wrong places, and in the wrong way. He said my naked body was as close to God as he'd ever gotten. I suppose that sounds foolish to you, but it made me so happy. I liked being looked at. I liked this house. It was a kind of enchanted place to me. It still is. But sometimes, when Mrs English was here and I was cleaning the mirror or something, and he was looking at me from across the room, I wondered what if she knew I was here day before yesterday, in front of the fire, naked as a baby while he painted me? Nobody ever looked at me the way he did. And yet sometimes I thought he wasn't really seeing me at all. Not like the way people don't see servants. It was as if the more he looked, the harder he looked, the less he could see. He used to get terrible headaches. And he had this idea there was somebody lurking around the house.

RUFFING. Who?

JENNY. I don't know.

RUFFING. When did he tell you this?

JENNY. It bothered him especially the last couple of weeks or so.

RUFFING. He didn't say who he thought it was?

JENNY. Somebody just out the corner of his eye. Just at the window, then gone before he could get a proper look at it. Outside looking in, at first. And then inside.

RUFFING. Inside?

JENNY. The last few days, he was convinced it had somehow gotten inside the house.

RUFFING. It?

JENNY. Whatever or whoever it was. I didn't like it when he talked that way. He was a charming man, ordinarily, but it was like something weighing more and more upon his brain. It was very disturbing.

MCGONIGLE. Why didn't you tell us this before?

JENNY. I thought it would sound foolish. And I thought you wouldn't understand why he'd be talking to a servant girl about such things. Or anything, for that matter.

RUFFING. Did you ever see this mysterious person yourself?

JENNY. No.

RUFFING. And you have no idea who it might have been?

JENNY. I didn't think it was anybody. I just thought Mr English was working too hard on his book.

RUFFING. You're sure it wasn't your boyfriend Johnny Robey?

JENNY. Johnny Robey was never my boyfriend. He didn't like me. He liked Susannah Owens. She's not lame.

RUFFING. Were you in love with Johnny Robey?

JENNY. I had a small infatuation. But that ended when I saw he was just using me to make Susannah jealous.

RUFFING. Were you in love with Mr English?

JENNY. Of course not.

RUFFING. Don't lie to me, Jenny.

JENNY. I might have had something like that sort of feeling for him. But Mr English made a person uneasy, after a while.

RUFFING. Was Mr English in love with you?

JENNY. No.

RUFFING. He never made advances towards you?

JENNY. I'm a good girl.

RUFFING. Then tell me the truth.

JENNY. There were times when he would touch me. He would tell me to be perfectly still, and then he would run his hands along my body, first my face, then – other places. It was as if he was molding in clay. As if he was – creating me as he went. It didn't seem wrong while it was happening.

RUFFING. Did it seem wrong afterwards? Does it seem wrong now?

JENNY. I don't know.

RUFFING. Was he your lover, Jenny?

JENNY. I felt needed, more than needed, worshipped, in a way. You can't imagine what it felt like, for a poor, lame servant girl, to be worshipped. But then I began to realize that it wasn't really me he was seeing. I don't know who it was, exactly, but I know it wasn't me. You won't tell, will you?

RUFFING. I just want to find out what happened to these people, Jenny. That's all I want.

JENNY. But I don't know what happened to them.

RUFFING. Do you know what the word widdershins means?

JENNY. Widdershins is backwards. The wrong way round the church, like in the fairy story. Why do you ask me that?

RUFFING. *(showing her the paper)* Because someone wrote it here and left this on the desk. Did you see it there?

JENNY. *(looking at the paper)* I don't think so.

RUFFING. You're not certain?

JENNY. I don't remember.

RUFFING. You don't think you'd remember, if you had?

JENNY. I suppose I would. Please, if you tell them in the village, about the pictures, I don't know what I'll do.

RUFFING. Jenny, you allowed a man to paint you naked. What did you think was going to happen to those paintings? Didn't you think people would see them?

JENNY. I thought if anybody saw them, it would be far away from here, in London or Paris, someplace I'd never be, a long time from now. I didn't think Mr English would let anyone around here see them, and while it was happening, while I was in the middle of it, I didn't really think about things like that. When you're caught up in the middle of something extraordinary like that, you don't think about the consequences. You just live it through, in all its madness, to the end.

RUFFING. And what was the end, Jenny?

JENNY. The end was that I stopped posing for him.

RUFFING. Why did you stop?

ENGLISH. *(Appearing from within the house.* **RUFFING, MCGONIGLE** *and* **NED** *remain and watch, as before.)* What is it, Jenny? What's wrong? Have I made you sad?

JENNY. I was sad enough before I met you.

ENGLISH. But not the same.

JENNY. No. I was not the same.

ENGLISH. Do you not want to do this any more? Because if you don't like this, you don't have to do it. Just say the word and we'll stop. It's not a condition for working here. It's not a condition for anything. I would not wish to take advantage.

JENNY. I don't know if you've taken advantage or not. But it isn't that.

ENGLISH. Then what makes you look so sad?

JENNY. Is this all, then?

ENGLISH. What do you mean?

JENNY. I take off my clothes and you look at me and paint me. Is that all?

ENGLISH. What else do you want?

JENNY. I feel so empty sometimes. As if all touch were impossible.

ENGLISH. But we touch. I touch you. I've touched every part of your body, Jenny.

JENNY. And has it made you happy?

ENGLISH. I've upset you. I never meant to do that. Tell me what you want.

JENNY. I want you to see me when you look at me.

ENGLISH. I see you.

JENNY. No. You don't. You look at me but you don't see me. You put your hands on my flesh but you don't touch me.

ENGLISH. It's true I am of late a bit distracted. It's just that – you'll think me very foolish.

JENNY. I don't care if it's foolish. Everything is foolish. Just tell me what it is.

ENGLISH. I can't help feeling, when I'm watching you, that something is watching me. I don't know who or what. But lately I've begun to feel more and more certain that there is somebody just over my shoulder, just at the back of my head, looking at me. Sometimes I think perhaps I need to get away from this place for a while.

JENNY. Then why don't you?

ENGLISH. Do you want me to go away?

JENNY. No. I just don't understand why you don't, if this place bothers you so much.

ENGLISH. Do you never feel, when you're here, that someone is looking at you?

JENNY. Someone is looking at me. You're looking at me.

ENGLISH. That's not what I mean.

JENNY. Then I don't know what you mean.

ENGLISH. It's not really that I need to get away. Perhaps it's that I need to get farther inside.

JENNY. Farther inside what? Me?

ENGLISH. No. Not you. Well, yes, you. In a way. I need to get deeper in. I need to penetrate more deeply into, more deeply inside the nature of things, to the core of things, so I can see.

JENNY. See what?

ENGLISH. See what's looking over my shoulder.

JENNY. Why don't you just turn around?

ENGLISH. Because when I turn around, it's always gone. The only way I can see it, I think, is backwards, that is, by looking in the opposite direction, by looking more and more deeply into – I don't know what. Your eyes. Your soul. I don't know, Jenny. I know I don't want to hurt you, or upset you, or make you unhappy.

JENNY. Then perhaps we should stop. Yes, I think we shouldn't do this any more. I could go on, I think, if it just didn't make me so sad.

ENGLISH. Yes, well, that's how one feels about life, isn't it?

(He sits down at the desk and holds his head in his hands.)

JENNY. *(turning to* **RUFFING***)* You won't tell them, in the village, about the pictures, will you?

RUFFING. I can make you no promises, Jenny. You've done a very foolish thing.

JENNY. But I had to. Can't you understand that? I simply had to. Isn't it like that when you want to find the answer to some question, some puzzle, and you can't rest until you find out? Who took the diamonds or who killed somebody or what really happened? Or in love, perhaps. Have you never been so obsessed with somebody that everything they touch is given some sort of eerie magic, so you can't think about anything else until you've somehow touched them, stripped them naked and seen them, for who they are, for what they are? Have you never felt that, Inspector? I think you must have. You can't rest until you know what's happened to these people. It's a kind of fever in your head, a kind of madness, really. I had to do this thing. Only his madness was something else. I don't know what it was. But I think it must have been quite horrible. May I go now?

RUFFING. *(Looking at her for a bit. Then:)* I'll do what I can, about the pictures. Ned, please escort Jenny home, will you?

NED. Yes, sir. Come along, Jenny.

JENNY. They're dead, aren't they?

RUFFING. I don't know.

JENNY. They are. I know they are. Whatever it was, at the back of his head, outside looking in, it got in, and it killed them all.

*(She looks at **RUFFING**.)*

What's that?

RUFFING. What's what?

JENNY. I suppose it's nothing. For a moment there, I thought I saw something, just behind you. It was nothing, I'm sure. Good night, Inspector.

*(She turns and goes. **NED** looks at **RUFFING** for a moment, then follows. **RUFFING** gets another drink.)*

RUFFING. So. What do you make of that?

MCGONIGLE. Suppose the boyfriend is more attached to Jenny than she thinks, or than she's willing to admit to us? Suppose he's been hanging about this place, spying on them, suspecting the worst, and then he peeks in one day, over Mr English's shoulder, as it were, sees Jenny naked in front of the fire, becomes enraged, broods on it for a while, then returns one evening to murder her seducer.

RUFFING. Along with the whole family?

MCGONIGLE. They're witnesses. He must get rid of them.

RUFFING. So where does he put the bodies?

MCGONIGLE. I haven't quite worked that out yet.

RUFFING. A jealous and enraged young man spots his beloved naked before a married man, but he doesn't rush in and confront them on the spot, he waits until an evening when the whole family is home, then murders them all without a bit of mess, and disposes of four corpses in a matter of minutes, leaving no clue but a piece of paper with the word widdershins written on it?

MCGONIGLE. Well, perhaps there's a few holes in that hypothesis, but –

RUFFING. And what about the paintings? If he's spent all this time planning this brilliant crime, and figured out how to make four people vanish off the face of the earth, do you think he'd leave the paintings behind for us to ogle at? Not only would they expose his beloved to shame and ridicule, but they'd incriminate him as well, wouldn't they?

MCGONIGLE. Perhaps he couldn't find them. Perhaps he's insane. This is a terrible theory, isn't it?

RUFFING. I'm afraid so, Mac. Doesn't work.

MCGONIGLE. Well then, what does? We've got to come up with something soon. If those people are still alive somewhere, they might not be for long.

RUFFING. Yes, well, that's true about all of us, isn't it?

(He gets another drink.)

MCGONIGLE. Go easy on that, will you, Johnny? I need you.

RUFFING. Don't you worry about me, Mac. I am now well advanced into the labyrinth of a mystery, going deeper in, and it distracts me from – the larger labyrinth which is my life. Now, go and fetch that crazy woman from the tumbledown house down the lane. I want to talk to her.

MCGONIGLE. Old Betty? Why in God's name would you want to –

(ANN appears from within the house.)

ANN. Excuse me, I don't mean to interrupt, but do you people ever plan on actually finding my family, or have you decided to devote all your time to cleaning out the liquor cabinet?

RUFFING. Go on, Mac. Miss Howard and I have something to discuss.

MCGONIGLE. All right. But I'm not letting her bring those wretched chickens.

(nodding to ANN)

Miss Howard.

(He goes.)

ANN. Chickens? What about chickens? Do you now believe my family was carried off by wild chickens?

RUFFING. Did you know that Mr English painted nudes?

ANN. Nudes?

RUFFING. Yes. We've come across some hidden in the closets. Apparently the local antiquities weren't the only thing he was investigating. And the interesting thing is, the subject looks remarkably like someone we know.

ANN. Oh, God. I was hoping he'd destroyed them.

RUFFING. Then you knew about Mr English and Jenny?

ANN. Jenny? What's Jenny got to do with it?

RUFFING. If you didn't know about Jenny, then which nudes are you referring to?

ANN. He painted Jenny, too?

RUFFING. He painted you, didn't he? He painted you in the nude.

ENGLISH. *(still sitting at the desk)* No, I always had my clothes on.

RUFFING. My goodness, he was a busy little fellow, wasn't he?

ANN. I can't believe he painted Jenny.

RUFFING. When did he begin painting you?

ANN. In the summer before I left for art school.

RUFFING. Jenny broke it off, so he painted you instead.

ANN. I can't see how this has any relevance whatsoever to your investigation.

RUFFING. In my experience, naked pictures are always relevant, one way or another.

ANN. He promised me he'd destroy them.

RUFFING. Perhaps he did destroy yours. We only found Jenny's. Were you and Mr English lovers?

ANN. You are an evil, evil man.

RUFFING. So I've been told. That is not, however, an answer to my question, is it?

ANN. No. Certainly not. The man was like a father to me.

RUFFING. But Mrs English might have thought you were, if she'd found the paintings.

ANN. But she didn't find them, because he destroyed them, as he promised me he would.

RUFFING. How do you know he destroyed them?

ANN. Because you didn't find them.

RUFFING. Perhaps they're not here.

ANN. If they're not here, then where are they?

RUFFING. Perhaps the same place the family is.

ANN. And where is that?

RUFFING. I don't know yet.

ANN. *(as* **NED** *enters)* Then what difference does it make whether he painted me in the nude or not?

*(***NED** *stops dead in his tracks. She turns and sees him.)*

ANN. *(cont.)* What the devil are you looking at? Yes, he painted me naked. Mr English painted me naked. I was absolutely stark naked, right here on this rug. Do you have some sort of problem with that?

NED. Uh, no, miss. It's fine with me. I just – uh – wanted the Inspector to know that – uh – we have the uh – woman with the chickens here.

OLD BETTY. *(as* **MCGONIGLE** *drags her in, pummeling him about the head with a plucked chicken)* Hands off, pervert. Unhand my personage, varlet.

MCGONIGLE. Then just come along, and stop hitting me with that.

OLD BETTY. Come along, he says. Don't think I don't know what you want. You men are all as randy as billy goats in rut.

RUFFING. McGonigle, what are you doing to that woman?

MCGONIGLE. She seems to be under the impression that Ned and I are trying to get into her knickers.

RUFFING. Well, are you?

OLD BETTY. So you admit it. I knew it.

MCGONIGLE. I don't admit any bloody thing of the kind.

OLD BETTY. Keep away from me, or I'll throw a curse on you and wither your man-organ.

RUFFING. Here, now, Betty, there's no reason to be withering his man-organ. I just wanted to ask you a few more questions about this widdershins business.

OLD BETTY. Ah, you'd best stay out of that.

RUFFING. But I can't, Betty.

OLD BETTY. Yes. The rat is drawn to the trap by the stench of the cheese.

RUFFING. Why should I stay out of it?

OLD BETTY. You get in the maze, you can't get out. The thing devours you.

RUFFING. What thing?

ANN. May I go now?

RUFFING. No. Stay right here. Tell me again, Betty, about widdershins.

OLD BETTY. Three times widdershins round the church and the door will open.

RUFFING. What church? Any particular church?

OLD BETTY. The old church. The green church. A place sacred to the fairy people.

RUFFING. *(getting an old book from the shelves)* Like this? Here, look what I found last night.

(reading from the book:)

Cerunnos. The church of, called in these parts Herne or Old Hornie. Saint Nicholas is Old Nick, that is, the Devil. In Cornwall, Saint Nick still has his horns. Puck, the Welsh *Boucca*, from the same root as the Slavic *Bog*, meaning god. *Bog* becomes bogey, and the Scotch *Bogle*, little gods, therefore, evil gods.

OLD BETTY. Yes, all that and an old cooking spoon.

RUFFING. So the church one goes three times round widdershins is not what we would think of as a modern church, but rather perhaps an ancient holy place, where pagan ceremonies were held. It might even be considered, in Christian terms, a place of the Devil.

OLD BETTY. The Devil was not such a bad old fellow, once. But things got into his head. I saw him in the village, you know, in the guise of the drowned husband.

RUFFING. The drowned husband? Do you mean Mrs English's first husband?

OLD BETTY. Lurking about with a beard like nobody'd know him. But I knew. I could smell him out, me and the chickens.

MCGONIGLE. You've seen Mrs English's first husband in the village? When?

OLD BETTY. Last week, it was.

NED. I thought he was dead.

OLD BETTY. I see the dead more often than the living.

RUFFING. Where in the village did you see him, Betty?

OLD BETTY. By the town pump, at midnight.

RUFFING. What were you doing at the town pump at midnight?

OLD BETTY. Don't ask the old henwife her secrets.

RUFFING. You're sure it was the first husband, the one supposedly drowned at sea?

OLD BETTY. Sure as I'm a foxhunter. This house was his before it was theirs. It was her inheritance when he went under the sea.

RUFFING. Did he say anything to you?

OLD BETTY. He said, there's blood on the walls.

RUFFING. Where? Where is there blood on the walls, Betty?

OLD BETTY. In the fairy chamber.

RUFFING. And where is that?

OLD BETTY. *(looking at* **ENGLISH***)* Deep in the dead man's soul. Poor walking corpse.

RUFFING. *(to* **ANN***)* Are there catacombs around here? Or any sort of underground ruins?

ANN. There was a monastery in the middle ages. I do seem to recall something about the monks burying their dead in underground vaults or caves of some sort.

RUFFING. Where was this monastery located, do you know?

ANN. Close by here, I think. There's a book of local antiquities up in my room somewhere.

RUFFING. Could you find it for me, please?

ANN. I suppose. But what –

RUFFING. I mean now.

ANN. Oh. Of course. All right.

(She looks at him, turns and goes.)

OLD BETTY. I need to boil this chicken or she'll turn bad on me.

RUFFING. Do you know where the old monastery was, Betty?

OLD BETTY. I know the pot's boiling over in my kitchen.

RUFFING. Oh, all right. Ned, would you take Betty home?

NED. I'll do my best, sir.

OLD BETTY. Just keep your hands to yourself, handsome.

NED. Yes, ma'am.

OLD BETTY. *(turning back to* **RUFFING** *as she leaves)* If you want to find the Devil, look in the mirror.

RUFFING. Perhaps I will.

OLD BETTY. Yes, but too late. Come on, laddie. Off we go.

(She whacks **NED** *on the rump and goes out.)*

NED. Here now. Mind your manners.

MCGONIGLE. That'll teach you to turn your back on her.

NED. I expect a bonus for this.

(He goes out after her.)

MCGONIGLE. So. Where in God's name are we now?

RUFFING. He was painting the maid nude. Then he was painting his adopted daughter nude. He was studying the Druids and seeing odd things out the corner of his eyes, just at the back of his head, perhaps the drowned husband. And I must look in the mirror to see the Devil.

MCGONIGLE. I must confess, I don't see where anything here connects properly to anything.

RUFFING. Ah, but it does. Everything connects to everything in the labyrinth.

MCGONIGLE. You're looking awfully tired, Johnny. Why don't you sleep at the inn in town tonight? You'll get some rest, and the food's not bad, if you put a clothespin on your nose.

RUFFING. No. I need to be here.

MCGONIGLE. If you don't eat properly, you'll start having hallucinations, and then you'll be about as useful to us as Old Betty, seeing dead men at the town pump and whacking poor Ned on the arse.

RUFFING. I'm staying. I need the solitude.

MCGONIGLE. I should think solitude would be about the last thing in the world you'd need at the moment. It's sounding more and more as if old English was going a bit crackers out here with a damned sight more solitude than was good for him.

RUFFING. Well, then, if I can put myself in his place, and go a bit crackers in the same way he did, perhaps we can find these people.

MCGONIGLE. I don't like you being alone here.

RUFFING. Miss Howard will be here.

MCGONIGLE. I don't like that much, either.

RUFFING. What does that mean? You don't think she's safe with me?

MCGONIGLE. I didn't say that.

RUFFING. Then find yourself a lantern and go all around the outside of the house, check the orchard back there, and all the outbuildings.

MCGONIGLE. We've looked there.

RUFFING. Well, look again.

MCGONIGLE. What am I looking for?

RUFFING. A door.

MCGONIGLE. What kind of door?

RUFFING. A door to another place. The entrance of the great Miz-Maze.

*(**MCGONIGLE** looks at him.)*

Come on, Mac. I'm only mad north by northwest. You brought me here. Now trust me a bit.

MCGONIGLE. Yes, well. I suppose I've done more foolish things. I can't think of any, at the moment, but I know I must have. The door to the great Miz-Maze. Why not?

*(He looks at **RUFFING**, shakes his head, and goes out.)*

RUFFING. *(pouring himself a drink)* Son of a bitch is right. I'm mad as a March Hare. But it's here. The answer is here. Three times widdershins round the church. If you want to see the Devil, look in the mirror. Look in the mirror.

*(He goes over and looks in the mirror. **ENGLISH** gets up, comes over, and stands, looking over **RUFFING**'s shoulder.)*

ENGLISH. The Impressionists saw experience as light and the exchange of colored reflections. They distrusted a false, artificially superimposed symmetry, preferring instead an honest depiction of haphazard juxtaposition. And yet, of course, it was far from haphazard. The moment a human being opens a door and enters the labyrinth, his brain attempts to find or if need be invent the illusion of pattern, order, a chain of cause and effect, rules.

RUFFING. But I can see no pattern. It's all ruins.

ENGLISH. Well, what isn't? Monet loved scenes of dissolution: thaws, fog, mist, crumbling things. He did not perceive the artificial separation of objects. The real and the unreal mix. The saved and the damned are the same.

RUFFING. That is madness.

ENGLISH. That is art. The lunatic, the lover, and the poet, yes? And perhaps the occasional police inspector.

RUFFING. On a rainy night I wander here in another man's labyrinth, haunted by a dead woman, attempting to solve a mystery which is ever and always the same mystery, the one inside my own soul, the mystery of love and grief, the geography of loss, in the labyrinth of time and madness.

ENGLISH. I painted the image of the naked girl by firelight, again and again, looking for God there. But it was not enough. Looking was not enough. Making was not enough. Even flesh was not enough.

RUFFING. And so, what then was left?

ENGLISH. *(at the chessboard)* Would you play at chess with the Devil for his daughters? Look. Someone has moved the red queen. It's white's turn now.

RUFFING. I will not play chess with the creature over my shoulder. I must solve this thing. I must solve it. We have a vanishment. Some private demonology's at play here. In the dark tower on the hill, when the wife's away, the young girl naked in firelight. First the lame housemaid. Then the adopted daughter. Then what?

ENGLISH. Dear diary, she wrote. A red deer came to the back fence at dawn. There was a bumble bee in the house, precursor of death. A great black bird came flapping about the gargoyles. She took it to shoot rats. You're very clever. I can tell by the way you don't play chess.

RUFFING. Damn it, what have you done with them?

ENGLISH. It would be lovely, would it not, to have the power to turn time backwards, like moving the hands of your watch back, to touch a past time, and see what happened there? The time of Shakespeare. The time of the Druids. The time when a lost, beloved person still lived and breathed. The time your dead wife was alive, say?

RUFFING. Shut up about my wife. This has nothing to do with her.

ENGLISH. Of course it does. Everything does. You've spent your life making investigations into truth, you know one must follow the path through the labyrinth wherever it may lead, to the deepest part of the catacombs, the brink of horror, even to the edge of madness, and the truth is, Inspector, the reason you do so well with these odd sorts of problems is that you are more than a trifle insane yourself. The death of your wife has only brought this madness more to the surface.

RUFFING. You've murdered your family, haven't you?

ENGLISH. Well, you've murdered your wife.

RUFFING. I didn't murder my wife.

ENGLISH. You did. You loved her so desperately you neglected her to death. You were so busy chasing murderers in the labyrinth you didn't see the murder you yourself were perpetrating. You'll do the same to your daughter.

RUFFING. I am not like you.

ENGLISH. You're exactly like me. I am your brother. I am your image in the dark glass. I have been on the black pilgrimage, and I have seen it, just at the edges, just slipping around corners, what I could not quite catch with my whole eye, just at the back of my head. When I looked in the mirror, I could almost catch it, just over my shoulder.

RUFFING. What? What did you see in the mirror?

ENGLISH. I saw you, Inspector. I saw you.

(He turns and disappears into the shadows of the house.)

RUFFING. If you want to see the Devil, look in the mirror. Look in the mirror.

(He stands, troubled, lost in thought.)

ANN. *(coming in from the shadows)* Inspector? I'm sorry, I couldn't find the book. I don't know what's happened to it. Inspector? Are you all right?

RUFFING. The mirror.

ANN. What?

RUFFING. The mirror. It's in the mirror. The answer is in the mirror.

ANN. Inspector, I don't think you should have any more to drink tonight.

RUFFING. Widdershins. Three times widdershins round the church. Don't you see? They're in the mirror.

ANN. Who's in the mirror?

MCGONIGLE. *(entering, with* **NED***)* Here, what's going on? Have you found something?

ANN. He's gone mad. He's raving about the mirror.

MCGONIGLE. What about the mirror?

*(**RUFFING** heads for the mirror, puts his hands on either side of it, gazing into it.)*

RUFFING. The answer is simple. They aren't anywhere else, so they never left. They must be here.

MCGONIGLE. But they're not here.

RUFFING. Of course they're here. They're in the mirror. Three times widdershins round the church.

ANN. He's lost his mind completely.

RUFFING. *(examining the mirror)* They're in here. They're through the looking glass.

MCGONIGLE. John, would you like to lie down a bit?

RUFFING. Get away from me, you imbecile. Here. Look at this. What is this, in the woodwork round the mirror?

MCGONIGLE. Some sort of carving. Like a gargoyle on a castle, or a church.

RUFFING. Three times widdershins round the church. Three times backwards.

(He puts his hand on the gargoyle in the woodwork around the mirror and turns it counterclockwise.)

One.

ANN. What are you doing?

RUFFING *(turning it a second time)* Two.

NED. It's turning. It's –

RUFFING *(turning it a third time)* Three times widdershins round the church.

(A click is heard. He pulls the mirror open by the woodwork around it. Loud creaking sound. It is a door. Only darkness visible, steps leading downward.)

I think you'll find them down there, Mac.

ANN. What is that? How did you find that?

MCGONIGLE. I think you'd better stay up here with the Inspector, miss. Come on, Ned. Bring the light.

*(**RUFFING** goes and pours himself a drink. **MCGONIGLE** and **NED** go down the steps.)*

ANN. How in God's name did you know that was there? I didn't know it was there, and I lived here for years.

RUFFING. It was a simple but I suppose inevitable progression. First, the maid. Then when she refused to continue, you. And then, when you went off to school, the wife's daughters.

ANN. Oh, no.

RUFFING. He was slowly going mad, you see. His investigation was a part of his madness.

ANN. But how did you know? How could you possibly have known?

RUFFING. The mad know the mad when they see them.

FELICITY. *(screaming horribly, from below)* NOOOOOOOO.

ANN. There's someone alive down there. They're alive. What's happening?

(She rushes to the mirror door. **FELICITY** *runs up the steps and into her arms.)*

Felicity. You're all right.

FELICITY. NOOOOO. GET AWAY. GET AWAY.

(She breaks away from **ANN**, *but* **RUFFING** *catches her.)*

NOOOO. LET ME GO. LET ME GO.

NED. *(coming up the steps)* Here, now. It's all right.

ANN. Are they down there? Are they all alive?

NED. No, miss. I'm sorry.

FELICITY. LET ME GO. LET ME GO.

CONSTANCE *(appearing in the mirror doorway with* **MCGONIGLE***)* Let her go.

FELICITY. *(struggling to get away from* **RUFFING***)* NOOOO. LET ME GO. LET ME GO.

CONSTANCE. *(going to* **FELICITY** *and holding her)* It's all right. It's all right now.

ANN. Where are the others?

(She starts towards the mirror steps.)

NED. You don't want to go down there, miss.

ANN. What is it? What's happened down there?

MCGONIGLE. I'm afraid both your parents are dead, miss.

ANN. You mean they've been down there all this time? All four of them? But why didn't they cry out? Is someone else down there?

MCGONIGLE. Not that we can find.

ANN. I don't understand this. What happened to them? Constance? What happened to them? How did they die?

MCGONIGLE. They appear to have both been shot at close range.

ANN. Who did this? Constance, who did this?

FELICITY. It was the Druids. They came at the full moon to make the sacrifice.

CONSTANCE. Hush, darling. No talking now.

MCGONIGLE. You must tell us. Who killed your parents, Miss English?

CONSTANCE. It was a madman. He took us down there, into this very ancient basement, it's not connected to our other basement, you only get to it through the mirror, and he killed my parents, and then he disappeared into the labyrinth. The catacombs. There are tunnels, you see, all under the hill. They lead far away from here. He escaped through there. Probably you'll never catch him. Madmen are very crafty, I understand.

MCGONIGLE. You mean he's kept you down there all this time?

CONSTANCE. Yes. He just left, when he heard the secret door behind the mirror creak open. He said if we made a sound, he'd kill us, so we could not cry out.

RUFFING. Mac, you and Ned see about setting up roadblocks to catch this fellow. We'll need to cut off the place he comes out, first. Then get some men to come back here with you and follow his trail down the rabbit hole. And for God's sake close that door.

NED. I can go down there now.

RUFFING. No. You'll just get lost in there. Seal the points of egress first.

MCGONIGLE. But we don't know where the tunnels come out.

RUFFING. It can't be far. Go on. There's no time to waste. I'll stay in case he comes back. And on your way, send the local doctor here.

MCGONIGLE. All right. I suppose that makes sense. Come on, Ned.

(**NED** *closes the mirror door and he and* **MCGONIGLE** *go.*)

RUFFING. *(making sure they're gone, then:)* Now, quickly, Miss English, before they return, you must tell me what really happened.

CONSTANCE. I've just told you.

RUFFING. You've just told a lie. Now I want the truth, and I need it immediately. This is your only chance. If you lie to me again, I can't help you.

CONSTANCE. Can I trust you?

RUFFING. You haven't much choice, have you? Tell me now. There was no madman, was there?

CONSTANCE. No.

RUFFING. Who killed your parents? Tell me what happened. Tell me now.

ANN. Constance, tell us.

CONSTANCE. *(Hesitates a moment. Then:)* All right. Jenny had just left to get some milk. Supper was almost ready. Felicity and I were talking about our father – our real father – trying to figure out what we could both remember of him.

MRS ENGLISH. *(Appearing from within the house.* **RUFFING** *and* **ANN** *remain and watch through what follows.)* Dinner is on the table. Where is that stupid girl with the milk?

FELICITY. She just left a minute ago, Mother, and she's not stupid.

MRS ENGLISH. All servants are stupid. If they're not, they'd damned well better learn to act like it.

CONSTANCE. We've just been trying to remember our father. Why do you never talk to us about him?

MRS ENGLISH. He was a ship's surgeon, his ship was lost at sea, he was your father, and he loved you. What else is there to know?

FELICITY. Was he a good doctor?

MRS ENGLISH. There are no good doctors. He was no worse than most, I expect.

FELICITY. Do you miss him?

MRS ENGLISH. Now and then. Today I do.

FELICITY. Why today, especially?

MRS ENGLISH. I often seem to feel his presence here. As if he were still here with us.

FELICITY. Yes. So do I.

CONSTANCE. No you don't.

FELICITY. Yes I do. At night. I sometimes feel his presence at night. At least, I imagine it's him. Except there is something rather frightening about it. Was our father an angry person?

MRS ENGLISH. Felicity, you know, men don't like girls who ask too many questions.

FELICITY. Well, that's their problem, isn't it? I think women who don't ask questions are blind and stupid.

MRS ENGLISH. Like me, you mean?

FELICITY. No, I didn't mean you, I meant women in general.

MRS ENGLISH. Just what questions do you think I should be asking, Felicity?

FELICITY. Well, I don't know. I just –

CONSTANCE. Shhhh. Did you hear that?

MRS ENGLISH. Hear what?

CONSTANCE. Outside. I think there's somebody outside.

MRS ENGLISH. I don't hear anything.

CONSTANCE. It's like something outside. Looking in. Trying to get in. Listen.

(Pause. They listen.)

Do you hear it? It sounds as if it's at the window. Or at the door. No, it's in the house. It's right at the back of our heads. It's coming to get us. Do you hear it?

ENGLISH. *(entering, from within the house, with a black book in his hand)* Isn't that stupid girl back with the milk, yet?

MRS ENGLISH. There, you see? You thought it was the bogey man, and it's only your father. Well, not your father, but the man who's been impersonating your father. The imposter who's been sleeping in my bed.

CONSTANCE. Mother, what is wrong with you today?

MRS ENGLISH. Nothing's wrong with me. I'm perfectly fine. I'm always fine. James, tell Constance I'm fine.

ENGLISH. *(absorbed at his desk, writing something down)* Constance, your mother is fine.

CONSTANCE. You're not even looking at her.

MRS ENGLISH. He never looks at me. We're married. Why would he want to look at me when he has – other things to look at?

FELICITY. Such as what?

MRS ENGLISH. Such as this wonderfully fascinating book he has his nose stuck in at the moment. It must be an incredibly stimulating book, to be so completely capturing his attention. Just what is this book about, dear?

ENGLISH. Nothing that would interest you.

MRS ENGLISH. Oh, I don't know. You'd be surprised what might interest me. I have an interest in a great many things. I daresay you'd be quite shocked if you knew what I've been sticking my nose into lately.

(peering over his shoulder, picking up a piece of paper)

What is this you wrote down here? Widdershins. You wrote down widdershins. Why would you write down widdershins?

ENGLISH. *(snatching the paper back, irritated)* It has to do with some research I'm doing on the Druids. The maiden goes widdershins round the altar, and then is sacrificed.

MRS ENGLISH. Oh, the sacrifice of virgins. I can see where you'd be very interested in that subject. Are there pictures in this book? Let's have a look.

(She snatches the book away from him.)

I was quite fond of study at one time. I once memorized half my Quintilian just as an exercise in self abuse. Come and look at this, girls. It's quite fascinating.

ENGLISH. Give me that.

MRS ENGLISH. I'm just showing the girls. Don't you want to broaden their horizons?

ENGLISH. I'm not sure it's suitable for young women's perusal.

MRS ENGLISH. Do you mean you're bringing filthy books into this house? What has it got? Pictures of naked women?

(She turns a page.)

Gadzooks, it does have pictures of naked women. Look at this, girls. No wonder your father can't keep his hands off this book.

ENGLISH. Eleanor –

MRS ENGLISH. This one, you see, is Iphigenia, about to be sacrificed. And this is Jephthah's daughter, also about to be sacrificed. And here is a Druid captive, also, coincidentally, about to be sacrificed. My goodness, but these are very thought provoking books, aren't they, girls? I'm certainly getting provoked. Aren't you getting provoked?

ENGLISH. I'm getting provoked.

MRS ENGLISH. Well, it's no wonder. Don't worry, James. It isn't like they haven't seen pictures of naked women before, is it? These days, one can find pictures of naked women in the strangest places, can't one?

(Pause. She glares at him, smiling grimly.)

ENGLISH. Constance, why don't you and Felicity go on into the dining room? I want to speak to your mother for a moment.

MRS ENGLISH. Oh, I think they might as well stay. They know all about this, don't you, girls?

FELICITY. All about what?

MRS ENGLISH. Pictures of naked women. Pictures of Jenny, pictures of Ann –

CONSTANCE. Mother, please.

MRS ENGLISH. – pictures of Constance, and pictures of Felicity. Even Felicity. My youngest. My baby. You've been painting naked pictures of all the women in this house but me, and I want to know why I, your wife, the person by all rights you ought to be painting naked pictures of, is the only person in the immediate vicinity you haven't stripped naked and sacrificed on canvas. What about Old Betty? If I look hard enough, will I find naked pictures of Old Betty as well?

ENGLISH. Calm down, Eleanor.

MRS ENGLISH. But how can I be calm? I've just had the most wonderful adventure. I was cleaning today – I know that little slut Jenny is supposed to do the cleaning, but I make it a policy to always clean both before and after she does, and I was rubbing up this little gargoyle fellow by the mirror here, and to my great surprise, the little demon did a somersault, he turned, counterclockwise, and I thought, oh, dear, I've broken it, I have a real horror of breaking things, but then I noticed I could keep turning him –

(She does so as she speaks.)

– one turn, two turns, three turns, and then, lo and behold, a door opened, a door to another world, through the looking glass, this door had been lurking behind the mirror all along, and cool air was blowing up from some dank place which was not our dry, lovely little basement, no, someplace much older than that, and much darker. And I thought, my goodness, this is an adventure, I'm having an adventure, this door has opened into another dimension, just for you, Eleanor, so I took the candle and went down the steps into the darkness, into the damp inner chambers of oblivion behind the looking glass, and there I found the secret chamber of the Knave of Hearts, and many naked pictures of his tarts. My trusted servant Jenny, my adopted daughter Ann, my wise oldest girl Constance, and my youngest, sweet, innocent Felicity. Naked pictures of each one, all being sacrificed, naked, on the altar of a loathesome, evil god.

ENGLISH. Eleanor, listen to me, you don't understand what you've seen.

MRS ENGLISH. Oh, yes, I think I do.

ENGLISH. I don't think you do.

MRS ENGLISH. Yes, I do.

ENGLISH. This is part of my work. The girls agreed to help me. It was entirely voluntary on their part. No one was coerced in any way. It's purely a matter of art. And a part of my investigations into truth.

MRS ENGLISH. Yes. I'm sure it was.

(pause)

ENGLISH. So are we all right about this?

MRS ENGLISH. Oh, we're more than all right.

ENGLISH. What does that mean?

MRS ENGLISH. Do you know, James, that, one of the great advantages to being a wife is, on any given night, when one's beloved husband is asleep, one is in an excellect position, if one should ever so choose, to take a nice, sharp straight razor and slice his throat open from one earlobe to the other? Or, if one were in a more playful frame of mind, to simply remove instead some part or other of his male physiognomy.

CONSTANCE. Oh, dear.

FELICITY. I never thought of that.

MRS ENGLISH. You will when you're married, dear.

ENGLISH. I think we should all just –

MRS ENGLISH. But you see, James, I don't give a tinker's fart what you think. Another thing you might want to keep in mind is that by the terms of my inheritance all our property and most of our money is in my name and my name only.

ENGLISH. Is that some sort of threat?

MRS ENGLISH. I have no need to threaten a man the future of whose ballocks I already hold in my hand.

ENGLISH. Eleanor! Will you watch your language in front of the children?

MRS ENGLISH. Oh, sorry. You can gawk at them stark naked, but I can't mention your ballocks. I guess I'm a little fuzzy on the rules of etiquette these days.

ENGLISH. I'm sure that once you've had a chance to calm down –

MRS ENGLISH. Sit down and shut up.

(Pause. **ENGLISH** *sits.)*

What a good boy you are. Now, listen to me, Jimmy. As much as I really would enjoy murdering and/or castrating you in your sleep, that might be a bit impractical for a number of reasons, so instead we're going to have to find a way for you to pay for what you've done. Now, let's see. What can we do to make you pay? Oh, I know. First, you must burn all the paintings.

ENGLISH. Burn the paintings? I really don't see why that's –

MRS ENGLISH. SILENCE.

(pause)

In the future, you will speak only when spoken to. Now, if you wish to continue residing peacefully within the bosom of this family and the warmth of my inheritance, you will do the following: you will burn every painting you have done.

ENGLISH. May I at least keep the ones which –

MRS ENGLISH. You will burn everything.

ENGLISH. But some of them are landscapes. Some are of dogs.

MRS ENGLISH. You will burn the dogs, you will burn the landscapes, you will burn the seascapes, you will burn the portraits of cattle grazing peacefully in the meadow, you will burn it ALL, or I shall notify my solicitor and drop kick you out onto your arse with nary a penny in your codpiece, do you read me?

ENGLISH. All right. If you like, I'll burn them.

MRS ENGLISH. Also, your manuscripts.

ENGLISH. Which manuscripts?

MRS ENGLISH. All of them. Everything.

ENGLISH. But what's that got to do with –

MRS ENGLISH. They are a part of your stupid investigations, and they are going into the flames.

ENGLISH. I am not burning my life's work.

MRS ENGLISH. You will have no money to do your life's work when I throw you out on your pompous arse.

ENGLISH. Eleanor, if you try anything like that, I might be forced to make public –

MRS ENGLISH. To make public the fact that you have molested my daughters?

ENGLISH. I haven't molested them, I've painted them.

MRS ENGLISH. The one is by definition the other.

ENGLISH. It most certainly is not.

FELICITY. You're not really going to make him burn the paintings, are you, Mother?

MRS ENGLISH. You stay out of this.

FELICITY. But I don't want you to burn them.

MRS ENGLISH. You don't know what you want. Now, just leave this to me.

CONSTANCE. There will be no burning.

MRS ENGLISH. Don't tell me you want to save those filthy pictures too.

CONSTANCE. Yes. As a matter of fact, I do. Very much.

MRS ENGLISH. Do you realize what will happen if those paintings should ever surface in some art gallery? Picture yourself, thirty years hence, married to some respectable country gentleman, with a great horde of your own children –

CONSTANCE. I am picturing that. And, frankly, Mother, it's not a pretty picture. I should like this record of a time when I was young and beautiful to exist. I should like someone, at some time, to look at these pictures and say, my God, look at that woman, look at her, I'd die for her. That's what I want. Someone to want to die for me.

MRS ENGLISH. This is absolute rubbish. My God, how could any daughter of mine even think such nonsense? What has this monster done to corrupt you so?

FELICITY. But what about the sacrifice?

MRS ENGLISH. What sacrifice?

FELICITY. We have given ourselves up as a sacrifice. Like the Druids.

MRS ENGLISH. What the devil is she talking about?

FELICITY. We have given ourselves up naked as a sacrifice. Don't you see? It is the union of paganism and art. It is our life's work.

MRS ENGLISH. No, it's HIS life's work, and a sorry enough thing it is, at that, if you call it a life's work getting innocent young girls to pose stark naked.

FELICITY. I'm not going to let you destroy them.

MRS ENGLISH. I'd like to see you try and stop me.

ENGLISH. We can stop you, you know.

MRS ENGLISH. What are you going to do? Kill me?

ENGLISH. I don't need to kill you. I'm your husband. I can simply have you committed.

MRS ENGLISH. Have me committed? Are you insane?

ENGLISH. No, you are. You've been having hallucinations about Druid ceremonies and your daughters running around being naked sacrifices, secret basements behind somersaulting gargoyles, and things looking over your shoulder in the mirror. It pains me greatly, but your behavior has become so alarmingly bizarre of late, I think we might be forced to have you carted off to Bedlam. That is still my legal right. And then, of course, under the law, I would become the administrator of all your possessions.

MRS ENGLISH. You wouldn't dare.

ENGLISH. As a Druid priest, I would dare anything. What do you say, girls? Shall we toss your old Mum in the crazy house?

FELICITY. I think that's a splendid idea.

MRS ENGLISH. This is absurd. Constance, you wouldn't let them do that, would you?

CONSTANCE. Frankly, Mother, I've always suspected you were not right in the head.

MRS ENGLISH. All right. If you won't burn this sordid trash, I'll burn it myself.

(She heads for the mirror door.)

ENGLISH. Eleanor, get away from there.

FELICITY. Mother –

MRS ENGLISH. I shall burn the whole lot. I should have done it to begin with.

(She disappears down the steps.)

CONSTANCE. Stop her.

ENGLISH. Eleanor, damn you, I believe you ARE mad.

(He starts down the steps after her, looks back at the girls.)

Don't come down here.

*(**ENGLISH** goes down the steps, closing the door after him.)*

FELICITY. Why doesn't he want us down there? Is he going to kill her? Oh, I hope so.

CONSTANCE. Felicity, where is father's gun?

FELICITY. His gun?

CONSTANCE. Yes. It's not on the wall.

FELICITY. Oh, I took it down into the catacombs to shoot rats.

CONSTANCE. Do you mean it's still down there?

FELICITY. I believe so. You don't think –

(sound of a very loud gunshot from below)

RUFFING. Then you went downstairs?

CONSTANCE. Yes. We went downstairs. Apparently Mother was trying to burn the pictures. Father tried to stop her. She picked up the gun, and when Father grabbed her wrist, he was shot through the heart and killed instantly. Mother became hysterical. I tried to take the gun from her, and it went off. It blew a terrible hole in her temple. Felicity's been like this ever since. We were afraid to come up. We didn't know what to do. We didn't think anyone would understand. I suppose we've been insane. We feel it's our fault. It is our fault, isn't it? I thought perhaps then we should destroy the paintings after all, but I couldn't bear to, even after this. So I hid them, in the deepest part of the catacombs. Then, at least, perhaps some day, someone will come upon them, and know that we were real once. I mean, a civilized person simply does not destroy works of art. One simply does not do such things.

ANN. Inspector, is there really any need for this to become a matter of public knowledge? None of this was their fault. Couldn't we just –

*(***MCGONIGLE** *returns.)*

MCGONIGLE. The doctor's on his way. No sign of the intruder anywhere.

ANN. Probably he's gotten away. Or perhaps he's lost in the labyrinth of tunnels. He could die in there and never be found. Don't you think so, Inspector?

(pause)

RUFFING. Yes. I expect you're right. I expect we'll never find him.

MCGONIGLE. Can you give us a description?

CONSTANCE. No. I'm sorry. He said if we looked him directly in the face, he'd kill us.

FELICITY. I saw him. It was him. It was the person who was just always lurking around the corner, the person who was just out the window, outside looking in, just at the back of our heads, just there in the mirror, behind our shoulder, the one I have dreamed of all my life, the dark one, the one who goes always with me, waiting for his chance. I can describe him. Actually, you know, he looked remarkably like you, Inspector. He looked very, very much like you.

RUFFING. Yes. I expect he did.

MCGONIGLE. *(taking* **RUFFING** *aside)* What did you find out?

RUFFING. Nothing. They were too upset to be coherent. It was a madman.

MCGONIGLE. Something is not right here, Johnny.

RUFFING. Something is always not right, Mac. You can't have everything right. You can only strive for an acceptable level of incoherence. Beyond that is a labyrinth of tunnels leading to oblivion.

MCGONIGLE. You wouldn't withhold information from me, would you, John?

RUFFING. Always, Mac. Always. After all, we're old friends, aren't we? And on the subject of withheld information, there's really no need to mention the paintings in your report, is there? I mean, given that it was a madman and all, what's the point?

(Pause. **MCGONIGLE** *looks at him.)*

MCGONIGLE. Yes. I suppose you're right. Well. I'm going down and have another look, see if the fellow in the mirror has left anything behind.

(He goes to the mirror.)

Oh, damn. The door is shut. How the devil do I get this thing open again?

FELICITY. Three times round the church backwards.

RUFFING. Widdershins.

*(**MCGONIGLE** looks at them. The lights fade and go out. Just the sound of a clock ticking in the darkness.)*

NOTEBOOK: WIDDERSHINS

1

Pleasure inhibits new learning, unless it is learning itself which gives us pleasure. Thus the only way we can continue to grow is to nurture our ability to take pleasure in investigation. Investigation is a profound metaphor for human life. This accounts for the omnipresence of the private detective and the mystery story in popular fiction and in the electronic pulp media. These are pale avatars of the holy investigation into truth which is what, more than anything, defines the kind of monkey we are. It is true that most of these fictional depictions of investigation are simple minded and mechanical, but the fact of their continual reappearance is evidence of the strong if somewhat debased need in all human beings to investigate. Gossip, curiosity, genealogical investigation and the philosophies of Kant and Schopenauer as well as nuclear physics and staying up to hear the baseball scores are all manifestations of this insatiable curiosity which is built into us. Of course, this is the same curiosity which killed the cat, and it will also kill us, by and by, if nothing else does first, but, as with the cat, it is all a part of the game.

In small enough doses, detail has charm and beauty in and of itself and will suffice to show you God's face in a cracked old mirror, but after a bit you need more, need detail wedded to a journey, an investigation, pushed by the desire of somebody for something or somebody. And yet this quest of somebody for something or somebody seems thin and pointless unless the detail has charmed us enough to care, unless the looking has been hard enough at something or somebody so as to pull us into the mask and make it us, because the road deep into the particular anything leads us eventually to everything. Then we gallop along, desperate to discover what we secretly know and desperate for it all to be over and desperate for it never to be over or desperate to start all over again. It is not about satisfaction but about questing and detail and identification with the beast, the hunter and the hunted. It is all a wandering in a labyrinth which is the library of God's brain. And the road deep into the particular anything leads us eventually, by a commodius vicus of recirculation, back to everything. This is the secret of the quest in the labyrinth. The end of the journey is a mirror.

2

Nothing, says the supremely eccentric and always interesting Montague Summers, could be more crude than explanation. Science is about everything we can measure, quantify, discover things about by setting up controlled experiments. Art is about that, plus everything else. Art is particularly important for investigating that part of experience which is ambiguous, contradictory, unquantifiable, uncertain, unknown. It is about how people feel, about the confrontation of what they want and are afraid of and can imagine with what actually happens to them, and about the emotional consequences of that confrontation. Art is an investigation into truth as much as science is – the subjective truth of inner experience. Behaviorists often hate art or see it as frivolous or worthless or childish because they don't believe in inner experience, including their own. This is the terror and self-loathing of the intellectual sociopath.

3

Widdershins is counterclockwise, that is, backwards in time. To go round the church widdershins is to turn time backwards and inwards, as to the time of the Druids, to times of human sacrifice. It is the way you enter the secret chambers, and it is the way of the artist. If they give you ruled paper, said the old Mexican gentleman, write the other way. But to go widdershins round the church is to disappear. The writing of a play about an investigation is itself an investigation, and the investigation is always, somehow, of one's self. Any investigation leads one sooner or later to the back of one's own head.

4

The unifying image is *looking*, the protagonist wants to see truth, to find it by looking outward, then inward, and yet he becomes convinced, perhaps through his increasing suspicion of his own guilt, that he is being looked at himself, by this strange creature he cannot quite see. Who is this other passenger? Perhaps it is God. Perhaps it is the Devil. Perhaps it is himself, reflected in some dark mirror. In some strange sense, the person all the people in the house have felt looking over their shoulders in the mirror is the man who would later find them in the labyrinth, the Inspector himself.

Among the most frequently published and widely produced playwrights in the world, Don Nigro has continued to build a deeply inter-related but remarkably diverse body of dramatic literature over the years, work that is often mysterious and unclassifiable, employing a wide variety of dramatic conventions and styles of presentation. He has written monologues and epics, spare realistic dramas and surreal homicidal puppet farces, plays with music and verse plays. He continues to build the long cycle of Pendragon County plays, which traces the history of America through the lives of several related east Ohio families from the eighteenth century to the present, and features many characters whose lives are followed from youth through middle-age to old age in a number of plays designed to be presented in a variety of different combinations. Nigro has twice been a finalist for the National Repertory Theatre Foundation's National Play Award, and has won a Playwriting Fellowship Grant from the National Endowment for the Arts and grants from the Ohio Arts Council and the Mary Roberts Rinehart Foundation. He has twice been James Thurber Writer in Residence at the Thurber House in Columbus.

His work has been translated into French, Italian, Spanish, German, Polish, Greek, Russian and Chinese. John Clancy's production of Nigro's *Cincinnati*, featuring Nancy Walsh, won Fringe First and Spirit of the Fringe awards at the Edinburgh Fringe Festival, Best of Fringe at the Adelaide Fringe Festival, and has toured Britain. *Seascape With Sharks And Dancer* has been in the repertory of Teatr Syrena in Warsaw, and *Lucia Mad* was produced at Teatr Julius Slowakie in Krakow and the Teatro del Fantasma has presented a Spanish translation of *The Girlhood of Shakespeare's Heroines* in Mexico City. *Widdershins* was produced as part of the first International Mystery Festival. Nigro's plays have also been produced in Singapore, Hong Kong and Beijing, and toured India. SpielArt, based in Munich, has translated and toured two productions of his plays in Germany.

His work is produced every year in a variety of New York

theatres, and has been done at the Oregon Shakespeare Festival, the McCarter Theatre, Actors Theatre of Louisville, Capital Repertory Company, the Hypothetical Theatre, the Berkeley Stage Company, Manhattan Class Company, the People's Light and Theatre Company, Theatre X, Shadowbox Cabaret, the Hudson Guild Theatre, the WPA Theatre, and many others, in every state.

Born in 1949 in Canton, Ohio, Nigro grew up in Ohio and Arizona. He has a BA in English from The Ohio State University and an MFA in Dramatic Arts from the Playwrights Workshop at the University of Iowa. Nigro has taught courses in Comparative Literature, Dramatic Literature and playwriting at Ohio State, Iowa, Kent State, Indiana State, and the University of Massachusetts at Amherst. *Grotesque Lovesongs* was translated and produced on Polish television, and the film *The Manor*, with Peter O'Toole, is based on his play *Ravenscroft*. Forty-eight volumes of his plays have been published by Samuel French. The Don Nigro Collection at the Jerome Lawrence and Robert E. Lee Theatre Research Institute at the Ohio State University contains a growing repository for his manuscripts and other materials.

Also by
Don Nigro...

Anima Mundi
Animal Salvation
Ardy Fafirsin
Armitage
Autumn Leaves
The Babel of Circular
　Labyrinths
Ballerinas
Balloon Rat
Banana Man
Barefoot in Nightgown
　by Candlelight
Beast with Two Backs
Bible
Binnorie
Boar's Head
The Bohemian Seacoast
Boneyard
Border Minstrelsy
Broadway Macabre
Capone
Captain Cook
Chronicles
Cincinnati
Cinderella Waltz
The Circus Animals'
　Desertion
Creatures Lurking in
　the Churchyard
Crossing the Bar
The Curate Shakespeare
　As You Like It
The Dark Sonnets of
　the Lady
The Dark
The Daughters of
　Edward D. Boit

The Dead Wife
The Death of Von Horvath
Deflores
The Devil
Diogenes the Dog
Doctor Faustus
Dramatis Personae
Dutch Interiors
Fair Rosamund and
　Her Murderer
Fisher King
Frankenstein
French Gold
Genesis
The Ghost Fragments
The Girlhood of
　Shakespeare's Heroines
Give Us a Kiss and
　Show Us Your Knickers
Glamorgan
God's Spies
Gogol
Golgotha
Gorgons
The Great Gromboolian Plain
Great Slave Lake
Green Man
Grotesque Lovesongs
The Gypsy Woman
Haunted
Hieronymus Bosch
Higgs Field
Horrid Massacre in Boston
Horse Farce
Ida Lupino in the Dark
The Irish Girl Kissed
　in the Rain

Joan of Arc in the Autumn
The King of the Cats
Laestrygonians
The Last of the Dutch Hotel
The Lost Girl
Loves Labours Wonne
Lucia Mad
Lucy and the Mystery of the Vine Encrusted Mansion
Lurker
MacNaughton's Dowry
Madeline Nude in the Rain Perhaps
Madrigals
Major Weir
The Malefactor's Bloody Register
Mariner
Mink Ties
Monkey Soup
Mooncalf
Mulberry Street
My Sweetheart's The Man in the Moon
Narragansett
Necropolis
Netherlands
Nightmare with Clocks
November
Paganini
Palestrina
Panther
Pendragon
Pendragon Plays
Picasso
Quint and Miss Jessel at Bly
Ragnarok
Rat Wives
Ravenscroft
The Reeves Tale
Rhiannon
Ringrose the Pirate
Robin Hood
The Rooky Wood
Scarecrow
Seance
Seascape with Sharks and Dancer
The Sin-Eater
Something in the Basement
Sorceress
Specter
Squirrels (Nigro)
Sudden Acceleration
Sycorax
Tainted Justice
The Tale of the Johnson Boys
Tales from the Red Rose Inn
Things That Go Bump in the Night
The Transylvanian Clockworks
Tristan
Uncle Clete's Toad
Warburton's Cook
The Weird Sisters
Wild Turkeys
Winchelsea Dround
Within the Ghostly Mansion's Labyrinth
Wolfsbane
The Wonders of the Invisible World Revealed
The Woodman and the Goblins

Please visit our website **samuelfrench.com** for complete descriptions and licensing information

OTHER TITLES AVAILABLE FROM SAMUEL FRENCH

MY SWEETHEART'S THE MAN IN THE MOON

Don Nigro

Dramatic Comedy / 2m, 3f / Unit set.

In the first years of the twentieth century, Evelyn Nesbit, the beautiful, teen-age pin up and chorus girl, was the entrancing center of an explosive and deadly love triangle involving Stanford White, her married lover and the architect of many of the most famous buildings in New York, who liked to push her naked on a red velvet swing, and Harry K. Thaw, the wealthy, manic and demented roller-skating Pittsburgh playboy who married her, beat her with a horse whip, and eventually shot White through the eye socket during a musical performance at the rooftop theatre at White's Madison Square Garden. This wickedly funny play chronicles the grotesque events leading up to and after this notorious murder and Evelyn's wild, strange journey through her American tabloid nightmare as she is hounded by carnivorous reporters, threatened, used, betrayed, bribed, stalked and nearly destroyed by the rich, the corrupt, the violent and the insane. Part of Nigro's ongoing dramatic saga of America in the 20th century that continues with Jules Verne Eats a Rhinoceros, City of Dreadful Night and Traitors, Originally produced at the Open Stage Theatre in Pittsburgh and Off Broadway by the Hypothetical Theatre Company.

"Literate but quirky ... non-realistic theatricality ... smartly ironic ..."
– *Pittsburgh Post-Gazette*

"There was a bit of everything: wealth, fame, insanity, genius, and, in the middle of it all, a beautiful chorus girl ... The sensational story has been adapted for screen and stage ... but the latest play, Don Nigro's "*My Sweetheart's The Man In The Moon*," might be its most faithful version. It demonstrates admirable nuance and an impressive amount of research ..."
– *The New York Times*

"People who think Evelyn Nesbit is only a fictional character from *Ragtime* may find some surprises in Don Nigro's play, which chronicles the tawdry, twisted love triangle that "the girl in the red velvet swing" shared with master architect (and seducer) Stanford White and millionaire psychopath Harry K. Thaw."
– *Village Voice*

SAMUELFRENCH.COM

OTHER TITLES AVAILABLE FROM SAMUEL FRENCH

QUINT AND MISS JESSEL AT BLY

Don Nigro

Drama / 2m, 1f / Unit Set

Peter Quint is sent by his lifelong employer, the Master of Bly, to be the servant in charge of a remote English country house where Miss Jessel has just arrived to be governess to the orphaned children of the master's brother. The ultimately deadly love triangle that results forms a darkly funny and erotic Gothic love story. These are the lovers who haunt Henry James's *The Turn of the Screw*. Quint is brilliant, sardonic and angry, a man of great abilities trapped by birth into a subservient role he hates. Miss Jessel is beautiful, headstrong, troubled, and deeply infatuated with the master. As Quint and Miss Jessel's affair develops, the rivalry between servant and master builds to a frightening and haunting climax. This complex and hypnotic piece of theatre is by the author of *The Transylvanian Clockworks* and *Ravenscroft*, among many others.

SAMUELFRENCH.COM

OTHER TITLES AVAILABLE FROM SAMUEL FRENCH

RAVENSCROFT

Don Nigro

Mystery / 1m, 5f / Simple unit set.

This psychological drama is a thinking person's Gothic thriller, a dark comedy that is both funny and frightening. On a snowy night, Inspector Ruffing is called to a remote house to investigate the headlong plunge of Patrick Roarke down the main staircase. He becomes involved in the lives of five alluring and dangerous women: Marcy, the beautiful Viennese governess with a past; Mrs. Ravenscroft, the flirtatious lady of the manor; Gillian, her charming but possibly demented daughter; Mrs. French, the formidable and passionate cook, and Dolly, a terrified maid. They lead him through a bewildering labyrinth of contradictory versions of Patrick's demise and that of the late Mr. Ravenscroft. There are ghosts on the staircase, skeletons in the closet, and much more than the Inspector bargained for. His investigation leads into own tortured soul and the nature of truth itself. You will not guess the ending, but you will be teased, seduced, bewildered, amused, frightened and led to a dark encounter with truth or something even stranger.

SAMUELFRENCH.COM

OTHER TITLES AVAILABLE FROM SAMUEL FRENCH

THE REEVES TALE

Don Nigro

Full Length, Comic Drama / 4m, 2f / Unit set

A modern retelling of a spirited and lusty chapter in *The Canterbury Tales*, this addition to the author's cycle of Pendragon plays is set in 1972. The disreputable Reeves family has rented the decaying Pendragon mansion in east Ohio. Strange happenings begin to plague the family's crude and brutal patriarch and his angry wife, luscious daughter and demented grandfather-in-law as well as their two boarders, both lustful college drop-outs. Eerie colors appear in the yard at night, trees seem to move around, animals disappear and there is something at the bottom of the well. This funny and frightening work was first produced in New York by the Red Moon Ensemble and is part of the series *Pendragon Plays*

SAMUELFRENCH.COM

OTHER TITLES AVAILABLE FROM SAMUEL FRENCH

THE TRANSYLVANIAN CLOCKWORKS

Don Nigro

Mystery / 4m, 3f / Unit set

The author of *Ravenscroft* investigates the Dracula myth in a powerful, complex, darkly funny and utterly terrifying vampire play unlike any you have ever experienced. Set in London and Transylvania in 1888, the year of Jack the Ripper, it captures the erotic power and poetry of Stoker's novel while looking more deeply into the characters' souls to examine the sensual and frightening undercurrents of this captivating Victorian tale. Jonathan Harker has returned from Transylvania so profoundly disturbed that he is confined to Dr. Seward's mental hospital and Van Helsing has been called in to help unravel the mystery of Jonathan's dementia. Jonathan's version of events at Castle Dracula leads them into a horrifying nightmare involving the mysterious foreign gentleman who seems to be seducing the women in Jonathan's life. A complex labyrinth of fear, desire, violence and lurking evil spirals into a horrific and surprising conclusion. *The Transylvania Clockworks* is an elegant, original, subtle, poetic and exhilaratingpiece of Gothic theatre.

SAMUELFRENCH.COM